Come Back to Me

LESLIE HACHTEL

Also Available from Leslie Hachtel

Romantic Suspense
Texas Summer
Payback
Once Upon a Tablecloth
Memories Never Die

Notorious Series
Murder Most Notorious

The Dance Series
The Dream Dancer
Emma's Dance
The Jester's Dance
A Dance in Time

The Morocco Series
Bound to Morocco
Tied to Morocco
Freed from Morocco

Historical
The Defiant Bride
Captain's Captive
Hannah's War

Crossover Contemporary/Historical
Stay With Me

Acknowledgements

To Jena Brignola
for always coming up with the right cover.

To Jenn Bray-Weber for always making it better with
your wonderful and insightful editing.

To Bob for his eagle eye proofreading.

And to Judi Fennell who brilliantly does everything
I can't to get this story published.

And of course—
To my readers—
Thank you so much for going on my journeys with me.

The wind ever moves across the landscape. The trees, the ocean—these, too, are eternal. Maybe other things are, too. There is comfort in that.

Table of Contents

Chapter One

Leaning on her ancient green Honda, and tapping her foot, Skye Blaine waited for the estate sale to start so she could be admitted to the inner sanctum. Around her on the shaded, tree-lined lane, the maples and oaks painted colors onto their leaves and the air was just crisp enough to fuel momentum. This neighborhood whispered of money. It might have shouted, but that would be considered gauche.

The end of August in Memphis demanded clothes that didn't make the punishing heat and humidity worse, but Skye wanted to look like she belonged without trying too hard, so she had dressed in comfortable jeans and a nice sleeveless shirt.

Estate sales were Skye's favorite. Old things, their history embedded in the wood furniture, wine glasses or pieces of jewelry, sang to her, speaking of other eras. The people who had loved these things and used them. A part of her dreamed of being able to go back in time and see for herself. No doubt, that was what had spurned her interest in British history. It was as if the past held something for her that the present did not.

A whisper of breeze washed across her face and she smiled. The wind was a constant, not caring about the place or the year or anything trivial that affected people. This same wind must have touched the cheeks of men and

1

women hundreds of years ago and just kept on in a direction only it could understand. *Wow, Skye, just let that vision run wild, why don't you?*

But it was that rich fairy tale fantasy life that got her through the pain of her past and the slogging of the everyday grind.

Daydreams didn't hurt anyone and Skye wasn't crazy. She was well aware there were no knights in shining armor to woo her, or dancing at lavish balls, or attending court, but there was nothing wrong with letting go of the rational sometimes as a break. Which was what brought her to estate sales. She could picture other times, other lives, for a while before she had to return to her day-to-day routine. Skye knew that she shouldn't spend her life waiting for something or someone to save her. She was strong and brave. But wouldn't it be nice just once to get rescued? A girl could dream!

After what seemed like hours but was, in reality, only a few minutes, the front door swung wide. Skye walked up to the impressive entrance and strode inside. The foyer was just as she had pictured it, with a sweeping staircase off to the left and a ceiling that reached to the sky. The requisite crystal chandelier sparkled high above, looking a little less festive with an obvious coat of dust. Wondering momentarily what had transpired to transform this majestic residence from immaculately cared for to a little neglected, Skye eased her way forward into the house.

A silken yellow cord stretched across the bottom steps, discouraging any of the sale patrons from stepping over the privacy line. Skye didn't mind the limitation since on either side of this lower floor rooms were filled to bursting with all manner of dishes, glassware, furniture, and artwork. This was way out of her league.

The prices were simply going to be too high. But looking was free and she intended to check out every inch of the offerings. You never know.

Sidling up to one of the display tables, Skye carefully lifted a glittering crystal wineglass. The room's ambient light swirled in it, creating rainbows, and Skye conjured a formal dinner, gorgeous clothes and sparkling jewels, men in tuxedos, toasting their good fortune as they eyed all the beautiful women before them.

"Excuse me, are you going to buy that?" A man's voice harshly cut into her reverie. "Because I really need it to complete my set." His voice was sharp, unpleasant, peppered with a supercilious tone.

Hesitant to return to reality, Skye grudgingly handed him the stemware and moved on. She couldn't afford it anyway on her resident manager salary. Her rent was included, but money was still stretched. Her master's degree in history was within reach and she was trying to assure that student loans didn't cut into her future. And she was putting some aside every month for her Grand Adventure—Capital *G, Capital A*— as soon as she graduated. She hadn't decided what that would entail, but it would present itself when the time was right and she wanted to be ready. A little reward for all the hard work and dedication. And then? Maybe research or teaching? The potential was endless. Well, maybe not endless.

Nagging in the far recesses was the question that poked up its nasty head on occasion. Was she missing something? Was there a life she didn't have the courage to explore? Were the things she had laid out in a neat little order going to be enough? Like that old song… is that all there is?

Shaking the thoughts away, she glanced about the

3

space. An old gramophone made her smile, picturing dancing to a creaky old record. A dark painting of a woman looking down her nose at the patrons. But then, she would, whoever she was. More glassware, plates, serving pieces and a silver tea set on a tray littered table after table. How sophisticated and glorious! Afternoon tea with finger sandwiches and tiny iced cakes. Skye's stomach growled at the thought. And to complete the image, a lace parasol leaned against the table.

A Victorian fainting couch richly covered in deep burgundy velvet might have beckoned except for the ribbon stretched across it. There were rules, and bypassing them cost money. Skye comforted herself with the idea she didn't really like it anyway.

Next to the sofa, a huge cherrywood table squatted, its legs carved with intricate designs. It was large enough to accommodate at least a dozen people. The matching chairs—all twelve of them—were upholstered in a faded tapestry which had seen better days. Much better days, and Skye could only imagine the fabulous dinner parties, with multiple courses of exotic foods and scintillating conversation. Oh, if only she had been born centuries sooner. And so much wealthier. Or at least rich enough to experience some of the finer things that money had to offer. Or maybe just an aristocrat. *Silly girl.*

Moving closer, she drew her finger across the table, her face reflecting in the polished surface. She was caught up in her mental wanderings when something tucked in the corner caught her eye. A rolled-up canvas, forlorn and abandoned waited against the fancy base of furniture. Curious, Skye picked it up and carefully unrolled it. The painting whispered of ages past, of secrets as yet undiscovered. And then, when the subject of the painting was revealed, her breath caught in her throat and every hair on her body stood up.

As if in a trance, she studied him. The man in the work captivated her, nearly stopping her heart and tightening her chest. He stared out at her, stripping her bare to her soul. The room blurred, then disappeared, and it was only the two of them.

Slowly recovering, Skye blinked, steadied herself by squaring her shoulders, and more carefully studied the image. Red hair, long and pulled back. Eyes bright as the ocean at sunrise. The color was not clearly discernible, but she was certain they were a light sapphire blue. Strong jaw and well-defined bone structure. Handsome beyond mere looks. He was a man not ever to be denied.

Skye's mouth dropped open and she remained transfixed. Every thought, every beat of her heart, was in tune with his. He called to her across the vast sea of time, since the painting was unquestionably very old, touching her in a way she had only ever dreamed of.

His posture exuded confidence, with a tartan slung over his shoulder held by a brooch and kilt reaching to below his knees. The jacket he wore was a dark green made of what appeared to be velvet, which spoke of affluence. This was a high-ranking man in the clan, perhaps even a laird.

Totally unnerved not only by the man's visage but also the familiarity of it, Skye searched her brain to remember some elusive memory.

Visage? Where had that word come from?

Resisting the urge to sniff the image on the canvas, she tilted her head in wonder. Would he smell like heather and woodsmoke and horses and man?

"I can make you a deal." A woman spoke behind

Leslie Hachtel

Skye's shoulder, but the words barely registered. "Are you interested?" The female voice was persistent.

As the words penetrated, Skye jumped at the intrusion. Embarrassed by her reaction to the piece, but still holding tight to the edges of her treasure, Skye swallowed tightly to regain control of herself and looked up. The other woman was young, a twenty-something, and pretty in a self-important, "I have enough money to always look fabulous" way. Everything about her reeked of wealth.

"Who is he?" Skye asked, looking back at the artwork and trying not to sound too eager. Normally she would be intimidated by a woman like the one standing behind her, but she was so focused on the man she held in suspended animation, she wasn't the least bit daunted.

"No idea. It's an antique. And I'm sure the artist was famous." She grinned, showing impossibly white teeth. "But I can make you a deal," she repeated, a knowing look on her face.

"Do you know how old it is? When it was painted?"

The woman huffed with frustration. "I think it's from the sixteenth century. As I said, it's an antique. He's obviously Scottish. Honestly, I'm not sure even where it came from originally. I found it in the attic and I just didn't have time to have it appraised…"

Skye had been so spellbound by the man's gaze, her thoughts were foggy. She needed to pull herself together. Money was tight, but she had to have this painting. When she walked in the door, she knew this wasn't just a garage sale and she did have money set aside. The question was, did she have enough.

"How much?" she asked, trying not to sound too anxious. She knew the unspoken rules. Enthusiasm for anything at one of these sales let the seller know you were a sucker willing to pay too much.

The woman shrugged. "A hundred?" She pressed her lips together as if she regretted asking so little.

A hundred meant Skye would be eating nothing but salad for a week since she was valiantly saving for her Grand Adventure. But, hell, she could stand to lose a few pounds, right?

Tilting her head to examine the piece more closely, she noticed part of the upper portion of the canvas was torn, a small section was missing from the bottom left and the pigment had faded in several spots, no doubt from sun damage and the passing of years, but the subject of the work had managed to survive centuries. She could always have it repaired someday, but that wasn't the point right now. Skye indicated the damage and angled her head in question to make her case.

Keeping disinterest in her voice, although her insides were vibrating, her inner voice prompted her. "It is damaged." She hesitated for emphasis. "Fifty." She could get some bread and cheese to go with that salad.

The woman made a show of looking skyward as if she needed divine intervention, and then heaved a sigh as if it was a great sacrifice. "Okay."

Relief eased the tension in Skye's shoulders. She had to have that picture and she was thrilled she could afford it.

Gingerly, as if it were made of glass that would shatter at any moment, she re-rolled it, paid the cashier, and carried it to her car. Slipping it across the back seat, she was careful that no part of it was touching anything that might mar it further.

She uncharacteristically forgot about the other sales she had planned on going to and started driving to her apartment when her cell phone rang.

"Hey," her best friend Harper greeted her cheerily. "I know you're picking through trash today, but can we meet later for dinner?"

"It is not trash. It's treasure. You'll see. Why just today I found something amazing that will make you turn green with envy. And, when I'm rich and famous for discovering it, I might, just might, share."

Share? No. If she could actually ever meet this man—or even one of his descendants—she would keep him all to herself, even if Harper was her bestie.

"Whatever," Harper responded, tone dripping with disinterest. "Dinner?" she repeated.

Harper was Skye's polar opposite. Where Skye was sparked by her imagination and all the possibilities, Harper was cerebral and pragmatic. Skye wondered if Harper even read fairy tales as a kid. The stuff that inspired dreams. Skye did love her, though. They had been friends since Barbie dolls. Well, Skye played with Barbies. Harper did math problems for fun.

But Skye knew she could never resist showing Harper the painting, even if she was aware Harper would tease her. What she wouldn't do was go so far as to tell Harper how she intended to actually connect with this man—once she figured it out for herself.

"Sure. I can cook." Skye really enjoyed the alchemy of the kitchen. Blending ingredients and creating something delicious always gave her pleasure.

"Okay, great. See you at six?" Harper couldn't be bothered with cooking. Skye guessed it took time away from solving the next conundrum whatever that was. But Harper relished the process. It seemed nothing made her happier than when a column of figures added up or when an "i" was dotted, and a "t" crossed, especially if the letters had escaped to another page—heaven forbid and she had to bring them back.

Making dinner was no hardship for Skye, who enjoyed the process, so she was more than happy to make dinner for her friend.

She parked her car, picked up the canvas, and crossed the apartment lot, hoping none of the tenants would need her to fix some "emergency". That was her lot in life right now. As the manager for this apartment complex, it was her responsibility to keep the tenants happy without spending any money, since the landlord was tighter than a tick. Taking her responsibilities seriously meant she tried to be a problem-solver herself, and the renters seemed to know she would help them if she could. Or at least listen patiently to their complaints.

Luckily no one was in sight to waylay her today, so she carried her treasure reverently inside. Her apartment was small and cluttered with various finds from other yard sales that Skye had been certain would one day make her a profit. In the meantime, it gave her some interesting decorations to look at.

The furniture consisted of an old couch with faded floral upholstery, a wooden chest for storage which doubled as a coffee table, an easy chair with a rip in one arm, a scarred kitchen table from probably the thirties with two mis-matched chairs, one of which she used when she sat at the tiny computer desk, a bed, a dresser, and a few lamps. Not exactly feng shui. Which was why these weekend sales were so important to her. She could find lovely things at prices she could afford. And make the space her own.

There were no other paintings and lots of wall space. Chewing her lower lip in thought, she stood quietly for a while, looking around for the perfect spot to put it. The bedroom? Would she be able to actually sleep with the man looking at her? No, the living room was a better choice.

Light seeped in from the one window in the main room, so Skye had to be careful not to place the work where it might be in the sun and risk fading. She needed to have it framed, but that could wait. For now, she stretched it across her kitchen table and very carefully secured it at the corners with two paperweights and two mugs.

Heaving a sigh, and reluctantly tearing her gaze from the man, she moved to her desk in the corner and opened Google. She was a history major, and British history at that, so how hard could this be? Too bad she opted out of those art history classes, but…

She first tried to find the artist, C. MacKenzie in the sixteenth century. That actually turned up lots of hits, but without a first name, it would be impossible to narrow her search. She tried Pinterest and Scottish history, in an attempt to identify the plaid. The artist was a MacKenzie, but it didn't mean his subject was one. Tartans, unfortunately, were not specific to clans until 1739, so that didn't help, didn't bring her any closer to answers about his identity or even the era.

Staring at the screen until her eyes burned, she finally glanced over at the clock on the wall and was stunned. Four o'clock? Already? Where had the time gone? Harper was due at six and Skye needed to get to the grocery. But she resisted leaving him. Maybe she had something to make do with for dinner.

She scooted from her chair, walked over to the stove, and glanced back at the painting on the table. Again, she was struck by the power of the man. Just seeing his face made her lightheaded. How as that even possible? Grounding herself, she turned away to open the refrigerator. There was ground beef and the makings for a salad. Spaghetti it is.

***

"Knock, knock," Harper called out as she walked in the front door. "What smells so good?"

"Dinner you don't have to cook," Skye responded with a laugh. She handed Harper a glass of pinot and sipped from her own. Harper was all the things Skye wanted to be: beautiful, with long, lush blonde hair and blue eyes, confident, with an innate sense of style, and cool. She also intimidated other people with her superior intellect and quick wit. But she had been Skye's best friend since first grade and Skye was so proud of her, with not an ounce of envy.

"You will make someone a wonderful wife." Her friend grinned and took a deep gulp of the rich red liquid. Following Skye into the kitchen, she stepped over to the table and the picture. "And who is this?"

"No idea, but isn't he beautiful?" Skye tried to cover the sigh and failed.

Harper raised an eyebrow. "A little old for you, don't you think?"

"Huh? He looks to be about thirty."

Harper made a noise somewhere between a snort and a cough. "And when was this done? Two, three, four hundred years ago?" She giggled. "I must say he's aged well."

Shaking her head, Skye dismissed the comment. "Look at those eyes, the long reddish hair, and the

11

chiseled jaw. I bet the eyes are blue. And not just blue. Sapphire."

"Skye, honey, is this the beginning of another one of your fairy tales?"

Skye set her jaw. "I intend to find him and then marry him." *Many a truth...*

"Okay. And then you can settle down and raise unicorns. No wait. What was it you always dreamed of? Finding your prince and becoming a princess?"

"Funny. No. I always wanted to be the wife of a warrior."

"Warrior, prince. Honey, it's all the same fantasy."

Skye made a growling sound and strode over to check on dinner.

Harper moved closer to the painting and cocked her head. "Where did you get him? The picture, I mean. It really appears authentic."

"An estate sale. The woman didn't think he had much value. Can you imagine?"

"It's definitely very old. Done, no doubt after 1500, since canvas wasn't used until later than that, but the paint itself looks like tempera. They made it with egg yolks and pigment."

"How do you know all that?" Skye asked.

"Just because I deal in numbers all day doesn't mean I'm completely ignorant about art."

"I'm impressed."

"You aren't really serious about all this, are you?" Harper clasped her hands together. "Skye, honey, just because you study history doesn't mean you can actually live it. Time travel is nothing but fiction."

"I know you don't believe in any of that stuff, but I do. I intend to find out when this was painted, and where, and I am going to go wherever I need to so I can get answers."

12

Harper snorted. "I believe you." Although it was clear she thought Skye had at least one screw loose.

"How can you find out the actual age of a piece of art? I've been racking my brain all afternoon."

Harper shrugged, a sly smile curving her lips. "Carbon dating? I don't know. A museum?" She moved over to get a closer look and lifted the paperweight on the lower right-hand corner, looking under it. "Maybe 1562. By the background, I would guess late spring or early summer."

Skye was nonplussed. "But how...?"

Harper sighed. "I'm a genius."

"Are you messing with me?"

"No, I am a genius." Her grin widened. "Oh, how did I figure it out? The year is written right here. Come see."

"Seriously?" Skye ran over to her friend and angled her head. Sure enough, there it was. And there was a date scrawled below the name. "Oh, my God, you are a genius." She shook her head in disbelief. How could she have missed that? At least the artist's name was written on the front. "What about the one who painted it? C. MacKenzie?"

"Never heard of him."

"Well, he had a lot of talent. I wonder why he never got famous." Skye carefully replaced the paperweight and tilted her head. *Intertwining mysteries, but I will figure out who was the artist and more importantly, who was the subject.*

"Ah, the story of so many creative people." Harper pressed her lips together. "Speaking of... can we eat. I have something I want to talk to you about."

"Time travel?" Skye's tone was hopeful.

"No. Unicorns." Harper rolled her eyes. "Come on, I'll help you move him and set the table and we can talk."

"Be careful with him. He might just be my husband."

13

Harper *tsked* and carefully moved the painting to the coffee table, where it rolled closed again. Skye hurried over to make sure he was still undamaged.

"I was careful. I promise. You can move him back after we eat, okay?"

"So tell me what's up." Skye handed her silverware and poured two more glasses of red wine. They each took a sip and, when the pasta was dished up and placed on the table, Harper was ready to talk. "Jeff asked me out."

"Jeff? Do I know him?"

"The guy from risk management. I'm sure I've mentioned him."

Skye was forcing herself to keep her mind on what Harper was saying but thinking about the man in the picture kept sneaking into her consciousness. She shook her head to free herself from his grasp. "Oh, sure, Jeff. You said he was cute. But I thought he was married."

"He was. But he's divorced and…"

"And?"

"And he asked me to dinner. And I was so caught off guard, I said yes."

"That's fantastic. What's he like?"

"Well, we have a lot in common. We haven't had too much time to actually talk, but he likes crossword puzzles and photography. He said he likes my mind and then he asked me if I liked to hike and camp, since it's a great way to take nature pictures."

"And you lied and said you loved the great outdoors."

"I wouldn't say lied exactly. I can go outside."

"And your idea of camping is when there's no room service."

"Very funny, Skye. Jeff might convince me if the tent is warm and dry and there are no bugs."

"Good luck with that," Skye said, teasing. "But hey, he complimented your brain. That's nice."

Harper reached for her wine and took a deep drink. Slowly replacing the glass on the table, she looked up. "Do you think I'm boring?"

"No. I think you are pragmatic and funny. I'm boring." Skye dropped her head to her chest.

"You are not."

"You only say that because you're my friend. I *am* boring. Ask my exes".

"The boyfriends you've had were all stupid and self-involved and as for your last one…" Harper tilted her head, trying to remember.

"Andy," Skye prompted.

"Oh, yeah, Andy. He was gay. He was using you as a beard to go to the company party since he wasn't ready to come out." Harper huffed a sigh. "You just never found the right one."

"Why in God's name would you think you are boring?" Skye asked her friend, surprised by the question.

Harper huffed a breath. "I'm so in my head. And I took a good long look in the mirror before coming over here. My clothes are plain, my hair is dull, and my complexion is pale."

Skye grinned at her friend. "You are brilliant and gorgeous. You have lush blonde hair most women would kill for. Your eyes are a fantastic shade of blue and your skin is like satin. Where has all this self-doubt come from? You have a wonderful sense of style and usually your confidence just oozes. What's going on?"

"The divorce. I was sure it was the right thing to do. Richard wasn't even nice to me, and his constant criticism wore me down. It got to me, I guess. And now, I think I'm just afraid of getting on the dating merry-go-round."

"Richard didn't deserve you. He took so much more than he gave and don't you dare let him have any more power over you or your self-esteem. Any man would be lucky to spend time with you."

"You have to say those things. You're my bestie."

"No. I'm your bestie because I believe what I just said."

Harper stood and wrapped her arms around Skye's shoulders. "I love you."

"Back at you. Now sit down and eat this wonderful dinner. And tell me more about this Jeff."

"He is good-looking in a bookish sort of way. I mean, I don't know that much about him. I already told you he likes to go outside, but I am hoping he likes indoor sports, too. And he is very flattering. He tells me all the time I look nice. So... what do you think?"

"How long has he been divorced?"

"Well, just. But they were separated for a long time."

"So, he's over it?"

"Does anyone ever get over it completely? I mean, you commit to a person and then they cheat on you. It's a hard thing to get beyond."

"Well, I think a nice dinner and a little wine is just what the doctor ordered. And getting out there is a very healthy thing to do. Especially with someone who's nice to you. And since he asked you for a date, you should definitely have jumped at it."

"Will you go shopping with me tomorrow?" Harper asked. "I need some new clothes. I can't wear anything in my closet."

"Shopping?" Skye gasped. "Oh, no. Torture." Her grin belied her words. One of their favorite activities was spending time wandering through stores, buying, looking, trying things on.

"Oh stop. Is that a yes?"

Skye grinned. "Only if we can talk about—you know."

"Your imaginary lover?" Harper teased. "Sure. I like fairy tales as much as the next person."

"No you don't. But I can't explain it. It's as if he is reaching to me across the centuries. He's so real to me."

***

After they made their plans to meet in the morning, and Harper left, Skye cleaned off the kitchen table and spread the painting out again. God, he was so amazing. It was almost as if she could feel his presence.

She poured herself another half-glass of wine and sat down beside the painting. He was real. He had lived and breathed and had a life. Yes, it was hundreds of years ago, but what was time? If you really loved someone, really loved them, couldn't that transcend years?

There was no denying Skye felt as if she slogged through life, as if every day was groundhog day. She would get her masters and move on to what? She longed for, was almost desperate for, something new and exciting to look forward to that would get her blood pumping. Something different. And it was as if finding this portrait was the key and she had no intention of letting go. But Harper didn't need to know just how far Skye would actually go to follow this possibility.

Sleep eluded her and the shifting light on the bedroom wall mocked her: *we shadows aren't asleep, why should you be?* Almost reluctantly, Skye slid from the bed and eased her way into the kitchen. Flipping on the light, she walked back to the table where the painting waited. Standing over the portrait, hungry for some affirmation, she stared until the image blurred and she had to shake her head to clear it. His eyes revealed so little and yet so much. *I have to find you. But can I? Is time travel possible?* Einstein thought so. He even named it 'time dilation'. And who was she to doubt old Albert?

Maybe Harper was right and it had become an instant obsession. Skye preferred to think of it as an irresistible force, drawing her in deeper. She couldn't shake the image of that face now burned into her brain. And how could she? She knew that visage as intimately as her own. Was it possible she recognized him from a previous life? *Visage*? Was she already going back in time? Maybe she just knew him in a past life. That was as possible as any other theory.

Confidence oozed from him, surrounding him like an aura. Behind him, a distance away, water crashed on jagged rocks, then tumbled down to the shore below. Skye could almost hear the rhythmic pulsing. It was if he waited for her. Her bones resonated with his call.

Every time she stared at his face, there was some new detail to discover. But he was still as elusive as the wind. What would it hurt to do some research into the possibilities?

Skye had never traveled much beyond her home state. Europe was someplace she heard about but she had no real-world experience. And Scotland? The land of the moors and clans and rebellion and romance. Even now, just the thought of going there set her heart racing. But she had to believe it was possible. As crazy as the notion was.

But what about hundreds of years ago? What would it have been like? Living in a castle without any modern conveniences, in a time when people actually talked to each other. She huffed a laugh. It would be wonderful.

Well, the reality was it was probably not very hygienic, and the hardships were unimaginable when even the simplest tasks like cooking and laundry were a day-long affair. It would be harder than her life now, but in a totally different way.

What if she could really go there? Instinctively, her fingers reached out and traced the landscape. Could she meet the man in the portrait? Fall in love? Oh hell, that would be the easy part. The challenge would be having him fall in love with her. Was she even loveable?

She had just chastised Harper about the self-esteem issues. She couldn't let all that self-doubt stop her from trying for something that was likely unattainable. What was the expression? May your reach exceed your grasp?

Skye decided to go about this logically. Well, as logically as something this illogical allowed. If her actual intent was to try and span the years to actually meet him, she should start by discovering what daily life would be like in Scotland in the sixteenth century.

It had been an easy Google search to find the period-correct clothing. She would need a chemise, a partlet, which was the fabric that covered the chemise on the sides at the top. Then a stomacher, the triangular piece that held together the front of the dress, a kirtle or underskirt. And a farthingale, which looked like a strange birdcage attached at the waist. Petticoats would work instead. The prices were not enough to make her tighten the muscles on her neck, so she chose two gowns. Truth be told, she had enough money set aside. She had just not been willing to part with it. Without taking the time to analyze the ramifications here, she clicked the 'Buy Now' button. Soon those clothes would be winging their way to her, and she could literally try them on to see how it felt.

She was worried that her choices may not be exactly the appropriate styles. They might be out of date. But then, a smile lifted her lips. She needed a cover story and if she said she was coming from France—that would account for a difference in fashions. It wasn't like they could check. How likely would it be that someone from another country would be residing at the castle. Most people in the sixteenth century never traveled more than a few miles from the place of their birth. Fingers crossed.

Time travel—now that had been another matter entirely. A few hours of research and she was even more frustrated. Apparently, if the authors were to be believed, one could move from era to era by slipping through a tree, by chanting at ancient ruins, by touching an object from that time, or even by sitting in a chair in a tight closet. Since she had none of those possibilities, there was only one choice left: Ebay.

Ebay sold everything, so why not a conduit to pass through time?

And, after a search with all the keywords she could come up with, there it was. A cloak that gifted the wearer with the ability Skye desired.

The full moon will guide your passage. Take only what you absolutely need. Find the place lit by moonlight and wrap yourself in the cloak. And believe with everything in you. Then sleep. In the morning, act as if you belonged there.

It was as if the words were speaking directly to her. Why, it even came with a guarantee. But the price… $6,000.00 or best offer. Did she imagine such a magic garment would be had at a bargain price? Why $6K was almost reasonable if it actually worked.

The rational side of her cautioned this was, as

20

Harper would say, crazy. Her emotional side argued if she could get them to take $5,000.00, she could use the savings she'd set aside for tuition and her Grand Adventure. That was almost all she had in the world. And if she failed— if it failed—she would be left with nothing. No money, no dreams, no future. But it did come with a money back guarantee, right?

Skye stood and moved to the portrait. *I know this is nuts. I get it. But every fiber of my being aches to be there, with him.*

He looked back at her with his piercing gaze, as if to say, "no guts, no glory." He wouldn't say anything like that. But he might express some sentiment like it.

Almost as if a force outside herself moved her, she sat back down at the computer. Her fingers hovered over the keys before she made the offer. Her heart pounding into her ribs, her breath coming in tight gasps, she slumped down in her chair and waited. The seller had twenty-four hours to respond, but Skye sensed it wouldn't take anywhere near that long.

She jumped up from her seat and paced from room to room, then headed back into the kitchen for the bottle of white wine she kept in the refrigerator door. The cold bottle tingled against her palm as she lifted it to her mouth, not bothering with a glass, and took a swallow of the icy liquid. A deep breath and she headed back to the screen, still clutching the bottle. Another swallow and more pacing. Still nothing.

The guy on Ebay has twenty-four hours, she told herself. *May as well go back to bed*. But the anticipation and the repercussions from the risk she was taking would undoubtedly keep her from sinking into a restful sleep.

Crossing back to the face that beckoned, she wanted

him to reach out through the centuries and pull her in. She rubbed the back of her neck to ease the mounting pressure. *In for a penny, in for a pound.*

A ping from her laptop indicated an incoming message. Rushing to the desk, she viewed the screen. The seller accepted her offer. In fact, *offer accepted* shouted at her. Was it also a metaphor? An answer to the universe? The possibilities…

As if in a daze, Skye found her way back to her bed and laid down. The words *offer accepted* repeatedly twirled in her brain, a thrill mixed with trepidation, anticipation blending with abject terror. She was acting crazy. This whole thing was insane. But, if you knew you were insane, did that mean you weren't?

Deep in her soul, she was more than eager for something in her life that filled in the gaps. Love, security, excitement. But was living a fantasy and spending all her savings going to give her what she needed? Skye had to admit she had no idea. But, hell, she needed to do something or spend the rest of her life searching, filled with regret. But did that include chasing an impossible vision?

Her exhausted body resisted sleep pulling her into the depths, her thoughts reflecting her disquiet. Until he stood before her with hand outstretched.

Chapter Two

Eilean Donan Castle, Scotland
1562

It was the dream again. Ian MacKenzie woke with sweat soaking the linen sheets and what might be tears in any other man's eyes. It was frustration, he told himself. The lass who visited him when he closed his eyes, her with the lovely red hair. He was certain her eyes were green, the color of a Scottish meadow in the spring. At his side, she fulfilled his every image for a wife: beautiful, kind, warm and soft, with skin like velvet and breasts that begged for kisses and caresses. He could only see her from the side, so he could never clearly see her features, but he knew she was magnificent.

Walking and whispering secrets with her, he had never felt so powerful or so brave or confident in all of his twenty-eight summers. And that was saying much. Yes, he was laird, but he was also a man and he desired her above all others. Why, he might even be happy to speak vows with her and he had never been overjoyed with that prospect before.

Closing his eyes, he pressed his memory. Was there a woman he had encountered who even resembled this lass? No. There was no one. But he was the laird and had an obligation to marry and produce an heir to follow after him.

He had determined after the Battle of Pinkie that marriage was a war he would choose not to enter—if he had a choice. How many of his fellow Scotsman had died, fighting to prevent a forced marriage alliance with England?. But he would never choose a *Sassenach* and certainly not a *Francach*. If he had to wed, it would only be to a Scottish lass. So was this magnificent creature born and bred here? Or, torment of torments, was she unattainable?

Would God be so cruel as to give him this vision only to crush his hopes when he could not find her? Shaking his head, he rose from his bed and dressed quickly. There was much to be done this day, as every other.

Entering the main hall, he had no sooner tasted a bannock and swigged some ale when Daimh, whose name meant ox, and whose form fitted the name, approached him. Ian smiled at the man. There was never a more loyal friend and defender, and Ian trusted him completely. He, too, could do with a wife. Most of the wummin were terrified of him, his size and his constant frown, which belied a heart that melted at the sight of a child or animal in distress.

"Laird, there are mutterings. Queen Mary is widowed and on her way to Scotland to claim her throne. I fear she willnae be so easily accepted among all her subjects."

"Do you wish to marry?"

The man took a step back at the question. "Laird? I was speaking of the queen."

"Yes, yes. I agree. But my mind wanders."

Giving Ian one of his rare smiles, Daimh shook his head. "I see. Your sister has been reminding you again of the need for an heir. And you do not wish to suffer alone."

24

Giving his friend a quelling look, Ian snorted. "Not at all. I was just thinking of you. Are you lonely?"

"Keeping up with my responsibilities leaves no space for worrying over details."

"You consider a wife a detail?"

"Do nae let Maisie hear you say such a thing," said Errol, Ian's brother-by-marriage. He had married Ian's sister three years ago and there was never a couple happier. They already had a bairn and had been trying for another. It gave Ian hope for his own future if he could find the right mate. The lass that haunted his nights.

"What about the queen?" Daimh pressed. "We might need to defend her sooner rather than later."

"Aye, I agree," Ian said. "Work the men an additional hour each day and see that our blades are sharp. We will be ready when the need arises."

Satisfied, Daimh strode off to hasten the men to the training field.

"The idea of a wife plagues you?" Errol asked.

"Daily. But I know when the time is right, she will appear."

Chapter Three

Of course she had dreamed of him last night when she was finally able to doze off. And as she dressed for her shopping trip with Harper, she kept walking back into the living room to make certain he was still there, watching her, pulling her in with unspoken promises. Wondering what his name was, she sipped her tea and, staring at his image, tried to read his mind. Coming up blank, she grabbed her purse and headed out to the mall.

Store after store and, after hours of indecision, which was Harper's normal MO, Skye was starving, and no outfit had been chosen. In frustration, she sank down onto the chair outside the dressing room.

"What about the green? It was cute," Skye suggested.

"Green makes me look sickly. It's your color. Highlights the red in your hair. But it makes my blonde hair and pale skin look like I'm just getting over some horrible disease."

"You have got to stop that. You are beautiful." Skye nodded in affirmation. "Can we eat lunch? We might have better luck with full stomachs."

"Great, Skye. You want me to try on clothes all bloated up with food." Harper threw her head back in frustration.

"If you are bloated, you won't have to worry about

the dress being tight after dinner on your date." It sounded logical.

"Do you think I'm fat?" Harper's tone was just short of a whine.

"Oh, please. You're a twig."

Lighting up with the compliment, Harper went back to the dressing room and came out a few minutes later in a striking little black dress. Striding over to the mirror, she twirled around grinning and threw her arms out to the sides. "Yes?"

"Absolutely perfect! But can we get the shoes after we eat?"

"Do you ever think of anything but food?" Harper pouted.

Skye shrugged, then pretended to look sheepish. "The Scotsman. I can't seem to get him out of my head."

"Food is a little more accessible."

"I wonder…" Skye lifted her gaze and sighed. "I need to find out."

Harper lifted her eyebrows. "I know you're joking."

"Am I?" Skye heard the seriousness in her own voice. "I think it's possible."

"Have you been drinking?" Skye could tell Harper was only half kidding. "Okay, I'll buy the dress and we'll get lunch. It's probably just your low blood sugar."

As they walked to the café, Skye mentally composed a list. They took their seats across from each other and ordered—salad for Harper and soup and bread for Skye.

"Are you practicing what you'll be eating in 1562 Scotland," Harper teased.

"I'm going to make a list."

Harper tilted her head in question. "Of?"

"First I have to find out the actual location. Then I'll need to prepare myself with research."

"Research? You're a British history major."

"Yes, but I don't know specifics, like Scottish words, Gaelic phrases, day-to-day menus, or the weather in Scotland in September. History doesn't really go into the minutia of life in the past. It is more interested in events and the people."

"Point taken."

"And finally, I have to actually get there."

"You mean like a time machine?" The sarcasm oozed now.

"Not exactly. But I have heard of other ways." Her secret was burning, but she was reluctant to reveal her special purchase last night.

"Sure. Heard of them in those romance novels. They aren't real, Skye. It's fantasy." Harper shook her head and narrowed her eyes, looking hard at her friend. "Oh my God, you're serious."

Skye just gazed back, determination clear. "I'm going to need your support."

Harper opened her hands, palms up. "You are my best friend, and I cannot deny you anything reasonable. But Skye, this is completely and totally absurd."

Releasing a loud sigh, Skye sat back in her chair. "Okay, say it is. So what? I have been so careful about money and so practical and steady forever. Never doing anything crazy. So, just this once, I want to tie on the parachute and jump out of the plane." Her voice caught as she swallowed her doubts. "So, I am going to do everything I can to make it happen and, if I fail, I will go back to my dull, uneventful life, no harm done." *It just means the Grand Adventure is sooner rather than later.* "Can you be my friend and not just make fun of me?"

Harper echoed her friend's sigh. "All right. I'll play. But nothing too out there."

Skye's grin split her face. "We need to start with the where. I thought I'd take the painting to the university's British history department. One of my professors, Dr. Jansen, is sure to be able to tell me where it was painted." When Harper didn't answer, Skye continued. "Since you found your dress and we can get shoes after lunch, we still have time today. Want to come?"

Just then, their food was delivered. Thanking the waitress, Harper rolled her eyes at Skye and dug in.

"I needed to find some clothes myself," Skye said between bites.

Harper cocked her head in surprise. "You should have said something at the boutique. I'm sorry. I was so caught up in finding the right dress, I didn't think you might need something, too."

Skye grinned, then pressed her lips together. "Oh, what I wanted wouldn't be found in any local boutique."

"What kind of clothes?" Suspicion tightened her voice.

"Oh, you know. A chemise, some hose with ribbon garters. Something in velvet."

Dropping her shoulders in dismay, Harper carefully placed her fork beside her plate. Raising an eyebrow, she looked Skye directly in the eye. "Seriously, don't you think you're carrying this too far?"

"Last night I did some research on the costumes," Skye continued, undeterred. "One gown I liked is a dark red velvet gown with embroidery around the neckline and down the sleeves. And the other is a deep blue. Both have a kind of corset-y thing in the front that comes to a 'v' below the waist. It's called a stomacher. Weird name, huh?" Skye grinned like a child caught with her hand in the cookie jar. "And, of course, three chemises, and stockings, and shoes."

"You bought all that, didn't you?" It sounded like an accusation. "And how much will these items set you back?"

"My credit card was almost at zero," Skye responded defensively.

Harper bit her lip. "And what else?" she prodded.

"How do you know there was something else?"

"Because we've been friends forever. What else?" Harper repeated, more pointedly.

Skye dropped her gaze, unable to look Harper in the eye. "A cloak," she whispered.

"A cloak?"

"It gets cold in Scotland in September."

"What aren't you telling me?" Harper pressed.

"Did you know that Ebay purchases come with a guarantee?"

"What kind of Ebay purchases?"

Skye pressed her lips together. "Ummm, time travel cloaks." She whispered this last.

Harper barked a laugh. "I thought you said time travel cloaks. Only one or more than one?"

When Skye didn't reply, Harper's eyes widened. "Tell me you're joking."

Skye cleared her throat. "Only one. Just because it doesn't make rational sense doesn't mean it's not possible." She could hear the defensiveness in her voice.

Harper angled her head, her mouth open. "How much?"

Skye tried to lick her lips, but her mouth was dry. "It doesn't matter," she said.

"Oh my dear lord. Honey, you were saving all that money for your grand adventure."

"This *is* my grand adventure," Skye insisted.

"Is it all gone? Your money?"

Skye looked skyward, girding herself for the onslaught. "No. Well, not completely."

Harper pressed her hand to her mouth. "Tell me you didn't fall for some scam and blow all your savings on this ridiculous fantasy."

"It's Ebay," she responded, her defenses sprinting into gear. "I told you. All their sales come with a guarantee."

Harper didn't even attempt to hide her shocked expression. "Oh, Skye. Why?"

Her nose tingled and her eyes burned with unshed tears "Because my life sucks. I have no family. You're my only friend. And I feel like an abject failure. So why can't I at least believe in magic?" It was the first time Skye had actually voiced this. But there it was. And it had been there all along. Magic!

Harper reached across the table and patted her hand. "You can believe in anything you wish. And you are not a failure. Just because your mother was… not a mother… and your stepmother is a bitch and she's made your father hateful, does not mean you should take anything they ever said to heart."

Skye swallowed hard. She was not going to cry. Pain from her father's neglect of her in favor of his new wife never stopped stinging some part of her.

As for her mother—she had climbed into a bottle after Skye's father deserted them. Skye was ten and her mother's misery permeated everything. The woman's rages were legendary, and Skye would still jump at the sound of a cabinet or door slamming. Sometimes, her mother would console herself with men. For a short time, while the affair lasted, her mother would be happy and tell Skye this one was to be her new father. But too quickly, the bloom faded and another dark cloud would descend. And when one of her mother's boyfriends grabbed Skye's bottom—Skye could still feel the sting of her mother's slaps, because, of course, it was Skye's fault.

After that incident, Skye came home from college at semester break to find her mother gone, along with all their possessions. The big orange eviction notice on the front door had left no room for self-deception.

Skye had salvaged her clothes and a few possessions, sucked it up, returned to school. She got a job to pay her bills, and had gone on with her life, determined to never sink into the abyss her mother had.

"Listen to me," Harper continued even more forcefully. You are young and beautiful. You've almost completed your masters in a field you love. Too bad it's not specifically Scottish history," she teased, obviously trying to lighten the mood.

Skye was not amused, but Harper kept talking.

"You are amazing. Look what you've accomplished all on your own." Squeezing her friend's hand, Harper continued. "You don't need to live in a romance novel to have a great life. Or find the perfect man unless that's what you want. But you do not need a man to complete you. You are whole and wonderful on your own."

The warmth of Harper's words soothed Skye but didn't lessen her determination. She decided not to mention she intended to take a semester off. It would serve to save her tuition money and give her the freedom to visit Scotland. She could always go back to school and finish if things didn't work out the way she hoped.

Exasperated, Harper raised her hands. "But this man is not real. I mean, I imagine he was once, but that was hundreds of years ago. I just don't want to see you throw away your future and your security on something that's no more than a fairy tale."

"I have to try. Just let me try. If I fail…" She shrugged. "And British history *is* Scottish history… they are linked. Dr. Jansen always reminds his students of that."

"Okay, but you do realize it's not practical." Harper conceded, dropping her shoulders in defeat. "Enough is enough. You have to face reality. As I said, this man died hundreds of years ago. Meeting him by traveling through time is a fantasy. Please. Please, I'm begging you. Finish your masters. Get on with your real life. The time for pretending has long past."

"Can we just go see the professor and ask him if he recognizes the castle. It will save me hours of Googling."

Harper just shrugged.

***

Dr. Jansen definitely looked the part of a professor of British history. His VanDyke beard and waxed mustache spoke of an earlier era and his worn jacket and rumpled shirt suggested he spent more hours in reading than in concerns of fashion.

"Thank you for seeing us," Skye said, striding into his cluttered office. Books were stacked everywhere, some laid open from obvious frequent use. Dust motes softened the air and the musty smell of old leather permeated. "This is my friend, Harper."

Jansen tilted his head in greeting and Harper smiled, her lips pressed together in an effort not to sneeze.

"I know you're busy, but I need to find out the location of this work and I knew you were the perfect person to ask."

33

He waved away the compliment with a flick of his wrist and watched intently as Skye unrolled the canvas. Knowingly, he nodded. "Why that's clearly Eilean Donan Castle," he said. "Fascinating. When was this painted, did you say? It had to be before the early 1900s since the bridge didn't exist before that."

"The bridge?" Skye asked.

"Yes, in 1919, construction began on the arched bridge as a means to access the castle. Before that, you could only get to the castle by crossing the loch. You can see the bridge in current pictures."

"The date on the back is 1562," Harper offered.

Squinting at the lower right corner, he pressed his lips together. "Hmmm. The artist is a MacKenzie. Let me check something."

Jansen angled over to a stack of books in the corner and grabbed one from the middle of the pile. This was not a man who relied on Google. "You know that castle still stands. You can even visit it. In fact, it's on my bucket list."

Continuing to riffle through the pages, he finally stopped and tapped his finger on the open sheet of paper. "As I thought, MacKenzies held the castle in that time. So, the artist was a clan member. And a talented one, at that. The level of detail is amazing, right down to the man's dog."

Skye peered more closely at the man's feet and, sure enough, a small dark terrier sat beside his master. "Why, I hadn't even noticed that before."

"He was clearly a laird or at least high up in the hierarchy. The brooch is very expensive, certainly not worn by just any clan member." Looking up at Skye, the professor nodded. "You know this painting is probably worth a small fortune. A preserved part of history. Wonderful."

Skye gasped. "Oh, I couldn't possibly sell it."

Jansen regarded her quizzically. "Then what are you going to do with it? Donate it, perhaps?" His tone was pointedly hopeful.

That thought hadn't even crossed her mind. She couldn't imagine parting with it under any circumstances. Maybe her feelings would change, but for now the answer was 'no'. She needed to keep it, at least for the time being. "Yes, Professor, I think that's a good idea. I will want to research possible recipients, of course."

"Well, I can help with that. I have a list of contacts somewhere here." He proceeded to move around the mountain of loose papers and folders littering the top of his desk. "Well, I will find it and I can get it to you in a day or so."

Luckily, his desk was as disheveled as he was, so Skye knew it might take some time for him to locate the information. "Perfect," she responded. "In the meantime, I will make sure to keep it safe."

Skye thanked the professor, and she and Harper walked out into the late afternoon sunlight. The fading brightness after being in the dim office was startling, but Skye barely noticed. Excitement ran up her spine and her insides were dancing. "Did you hear what he said?"

"Which part?"

"The castle. It still exists. I can go there. I can actually go there. This is going to be so much easier than I thought."

Harper closed her eyes and shook her head. "This has got to stop."

Chapter Four

Eyes burning from hours of research. Skye sipped another cup of tea and stared out the window at her limited universe. Well, not limited for long, if this fantasy turned out to be possible. There was so much to take in and remember before she left, though.

The first problem was finalizing the explanation of where she had come from. Ladies didn't just show up at castles in Scotland, knock on the door and expect to be accepted without questions or suspicions. Her story had to be solid and beyond reproach. If she spoke English, she would certainly be thought a spy. No, she would have to have come from France. And that was just at the time Mary of Scotland was traveling back home from France.

Finally, the details took shape. Luckily she spoke French adequately, but the Gaelic escaped her, so saying she came from France made sense. Fingers crossed, the MacKenzies would not be aware of any minor mistakes. She could say she was born in Scotland and her parents left when she was young, but she always considered it her true home.

In 1562, the soldiers garrisoned in France contracted the Black Plague. From there it spread throughout Europe, taking true hold in 1563. Skye could say her parents, who were of noble birth, fell ill and, since she had no other family, she was left alone. With nowhere to go, and the sickness killing so many, she decided it was the perfect solution to follow Mary and petition to serve as one of her ladies. Before she could reach the queen in Inverness, however, she was set upon and the men with her killed or run off defending her. Making her way alone, she ended up at Eilean Donan.

Knowing that the Black Plague would be the scourge of Europe again in 1562, albeit not as devastatingly as it had in the fourteenth century, Skye needed to take precautions. Carried by fleas from rodents, she would need insect repellent. And a course of antibiotics. It would be terrible to make it to the past only to be felled by a disease with such rapid contagion. Or lose her soul mate to the horrible illness.

Researching the illness, she found it responded to certain antibiotics. Checking her medicine cabinet, she found some doxycycline that had two refills available. Skye had suffered from skin issues a few months ago and the dermatologist had prescribed it. Convinced the breakouts were stress related, Skye decided against taking the medicine. Perfect. She would get a refill tomorrow and between what she had on hand and that, she should be able to save at least two people.

All she really had experience with were names and dates and battles and political implications. That was helpful and she knew a lot about Mary, Queen of Scots, but until now, very little about the practicality of how clan women spent their days. Posing as a lady meant she had more choices, but at the same time, she assumed she would be expected to know embroidery and dances and proper etiquette. Checking pronunciations and repeating was helpful, and she hoped her memory would sustain her.

The late afternoon sun was washing the grass and trees with warm light and keeping autumn at bay. It wouldn't be long before the greens faded away and were replaced by the myriad colors of fall. What would the fields of Scotland look like this time of year? It would certainly be colder and definitely greener, without air pollution and traffic to muddy the sky.

She was just going over the things she intended to take with her on her trip to Scotland when her cell phone rang. Mrs. Baggins in 3A.

"Sorry to bother you, dear. But the light in my kitchen just went out and…"

"I'll be right there."

Clara Baggins was a darling old lady and still mentally sharp, although she had to be pushing ninety. She managed to live alone, which was a wonder, since when it came to the simplest household repair, she was entirely helpless. Ever since the older woman moved in a month ago, Skye had been summoned multiple times to open jars or adjust the air conditioner. As the manager, it wasn't really her job to take care of maintenance, or do minor repairs for tenants, but Mrs. B. was so sweet it was hard not to want to help her. And *Baggins*? Skye wasn't even a *Lord of the Rings* fan, but it was an unusual name.

Skye didn't mind the interruption. She hadn't been out of her apartment all day and, as much as she was looking forward to what was going to be happening, she could definitely use a break and a breath of fresh air.

Grabbing some spare lightbulbs, Skye walked across the courtyard, making a mental note to tell Charlie the yard guy that the grass needed mowing again. He was not the best worker, but she imagined the owner of the complex wasn't paying high dollar for his services, either.

As Mrs. Baggins opened the door to her knock, the scent of lavender and eucalyptus assailed Skye, making her nose wrinkle. But it was also very comforting, the smell of a loving grandmother Skye had never known.

After a few words of small talk, Skye grabbed a chair to stand on and switched the dead bulb for a live one. Voila. Tragedy averted.

"Thank you so much, Skye. You are so good to me."

"It was nothing." Making for the door, the other woman's voice stopped her.

"Do you have time for a bit of sherry? I always partake this time of day and I would love to share."

Hesitating, Skye bit back a refusal. Sitting with this old woman for a few minutes would be nice.

Skye sat on the indicated couch and watched while rich brown liquid was poured into two glittering crystal glasses. They each picked up their drink. "What shall we toast to?"

Before Skye could respond, Mrs. Baggins answered her own question. "How about to magic?"

Sipping the warm cordial, Skye was puzzled and no little surprised by the toast. "Magic?"

Mrs. Baggins smiled. "Isn't that what we all want?"

Cocking her head, Skye looked at the woman's face. The skin was wrinkled and soft, but her blue eyes were bright, and her expression conveyed some secret she was holding back.

"Is there such a thing?" Skye asked.

"Oh, goodness, I certainly hope so. How could you doubt it?"

"Mrs. Baggins, do you know a secret?"

"Of course, dear. And I will gladly share it with you since you have been very kind to me."

This was one of those moments when you wanted something so badly you were afraid to even dream someone else might have the answer.

"It will work if you take my advice."

"What will work?" Could this woman possibly know about the painting, about her plans to go to Scotland and visit the castle in hopes of—what? True love?"

"Oh, please," Mrs. Baggins scoffed. "No need to play dumb. You've come this far, haven't you?"

"What do you know? *How* do you know?" Skye's heart was pounding against her ribs.

Mrs. Baggins smiled. "You are a beautiful woman. And you seem to always be so busy. But I know you are lonely. It's in the depths of your eyes."

Skye chewed her lower lip and nodded.

"Did I ever tell you my maiden name was MacKenzie?"

Shock made Skye jump in her seat. "Really?"

"Oh yes. And the women in my family always had gifts. Healing, the sight, a little magic." The old woman smiled, crinkling the wrinkles in her lovely face. "I suppose it trickles down, you know. Don't you imagine?"

"I don't know."

"It's time for love, isn't it?" Mrs. Baggins' tone was so gentle, Skye's eyes ached from unshed tears. "Let me guess. You have an inkling how to find him, but the devil is in the details."

Skye's heart rate increased even more, and her mouth went dry. Was it possible this woman actually knew? That she had 'the sight'? "I am just not certain how I can afford the flight."

That was the part Skye hadn't been able to figure out as yet. That and what her excuse would be for simply appearing in a strange land? And with an American accent. She had worried she would stand out like a sore thumb, but the woman smiling at her seemed to be reassuring her she would be accepted.

Magic? Had the planets aligned for her and this was yet another sign?

No. It was possible she had been eavesdropping at Skye's door? Yes, that must be it. Logic calmed the blood roaring in her ears. The warring in her thoughts. But then, this whole pursuit was based on something mystical. And it was an odd coincidence that Mrs. Baggins had been a MacKenzie. Was the world really so small and connected?

"It's an impossible dream. Isn't it? Or maybe all dreams are possible if you believe hard enough."

Mrs. Baggins rose and pressed her index finger to her lips. Her eyes lost focus and her breath became slow and deep. "You must be there in a fortnight, for he returns the fifteenth of September. And remember you speak excellent French."

"What did you say?"

Mrs. Baggins blinked and smiled. "I don't remember, dear. Did I doze off? I guess it's time for bed."

Before Skye could respond, Mrs. Baggins stood and ushered Skye out the door into the now darkened courtyard. Standing alone in the cooler night air, Skye wondered if she had just imagined this conversation. Too much of the sherry perhaps? But her mind was clear, and she was suffused with both excitement and joy. And a sense of urgency. So much for logic. There was much to be done and very little time. And there was still the matter of enough money.

Looking up at the star-laden sky, she wondered if he was looking, had been looking, up at the same lights hundreds of years ago.

***

The following morning was heavy with clouds pressing down and promising rain. The thick air needed a good washing and Skye had been pleased at the prospect of a milder day. But before she could enjoy a few minutes to herself, the phone rang and morning rushed by in a swirl of what felt like hundreds of complaints from tenants with things that needed to be repaired, replaced, or simply patiently and diplomatically ignored. Skye would not miss the constant chewing on her ear, if even for just a brief respite.

It was mid-afternoon before she was finally back in her own apartment. Shuffling into the kitchen, she prepared herself a cup of tea and a peanut butter and jelly sandwich, and sat down at the table. Her calculator, bankbook, and notes dared her to find an answer to her financial woes.

Nibbling her sandwich as she stared at the numbers before her, she tried to justify her insanity. If only she hadn't had to pay so much for the cloak. But then, without it the whole trip wouldn't be worthwhile, would it?

If she took off for a few weeks, her boss would certainly dock her pay, since someone would have to come in and take her place. Her final tuition payment was due and her credit card was almost maxed. She could hold off on the tuition if she intended to take a semester off and the credit card payments could be managed, but what was she doing? This was crazy. Time travel? Magic? Pathetic! What was that saying about sinking into the deep end of the ocean?

Raising the cup to her lips, she looked over the rim and noticed a small white envelope had been slipped under her door. With no idea what it could be, she stood and went over to retrieve it. Her first name was on the front and inside was what appeared to be an airline ticket issued to her. To Scotland. Leaving in ten days. But how? Puzzled, she stared at the ticket, trying to confirm its authenticity. It certainly looked real.

Skye couldn't imagine that Harper would do this and Mrs. Baggins was the only other person who knew anything. It made no sense. Was it possible the old woman wanted a vicarious adventure so much she was willing to help finance it? Did she spend some of her life savings to make Skye's dream come true? If so, Skye couldn't possibly accept such a sacrifice. And how did Mrs. Baggins know it was Scotland? Maybe because her family was MacKenzie?

Well, there was only one way to find out, so Skye headed out across the courtyard.

Mrs. Baggins swung the door wide and greeted Skye with a broad smile.

"Good afternoon, sweet girl. Can I help you with something? Oh wait, how rude of me. Come in, come in."

Skye made her way into the sitting room and slowly sank onto the sofa.

"Tea? Coffee?" the older woman offered. "Sherry?" she winked.

Skye smiled. "No, thank you." Taking a deep breath, she plunged in.

"Mrs. Baggins, I can't let you do it. I can't possibly accept it." She handed the envelope to the older woman.

Pulling out the ticket, Mrs. Baggins stared at Skye in what appeared to be genuine confusion. "What's this?

Skye shook her head. "You don't have to pretend. You're the only one who could have sent this, and I can't possibly accept it. But the thought was so wonderful."

"Dear girl, I have no idea what you're going on about. What is that?"

43

Skye tilted her head and dropped her shoulders. "The ticket. To Scotland. It could only have been you."

Mrs. Baggins laughed. "I thought we drank to magic last night."

"Mrs. B, there is no such thing as magic."

The woman's pale gray brows shot up. "No? Then how did this ticket appear?"

Now Skye was the one confused. "I want to believe. I do. But my friend Harper thinks I'm crazy and I'll end up hopelessly in debt and…" She huffed out a frustrated breath.

Mrs. Baggins sat down next to her and scooted close. Taking her hands, the older woman looked directly into Skye's eyes.

"Skye, I can see you haven't had the easiest road, but it has made you strong. Belief in wonders, dreams—that's what keeps people like us moving forward. You will always regret not trying. I speak from experience. You must try. Or one day, you will be old and will lie alone in your bed, looking up at the ceiling and seeing only that life has passed you by."

"But what about…?"

"You can always make the money back. You can always pick up where you left off in your life. But you may never get another chance at something wonderful. Because if you pass it by this time, even if you have another chance, you'll lose courage."

Skye grinned. "Like when opportunity knocks, answer?"

Mrs. Baggins smiled in response and nodded. "Exactly."

***

The gowns and undergarments arrived the following day. So foreign, so lovely. Skye quivered in anticipation. Soon she could wear these and not have people think she was going to a costume party. Hoping that no one is 1562 would notice the even stitches were done by machine, she knew she had no choice. She had neither the time nor the skill to make them herself.

The layers, at least, made sense and Skye couldn't resist trying them on and practicing how to attach all the pieces. Suddenly, panic gripped her. She had stockings but nothing for shoes. Rushing to her closet and rummaging around, she dug out an old pair of slippers made of velvet that would work.

"Calm down," she said out loud. "It's going to be fine."

When the package came from Ebay two days later, Skye could barely control her eagerness and anticipation. Her hands shook as she carefully unwrapped what she had to believe was her future, or rather her past.

Slipping the top off the box, the dark gray velvet cloak lay snuggled into a wrapping of pale tissue paper. Nestled on top was a small envelope. Her breathing coming in quick spurts, Skye pulled out the note inside.

Dear Skye,

You have purchased a very special item. Its power is the things dreams are made of. You must respect that power and use it carefully. You are clearly a believer in magic. Hold that to your heart. Do not doubt or the process will most certainly fail. The instructions are as follows: When you have reached your physical destination (in the present time), wrap yourself in its folds. Whatever you are holding in your arms will go with you. Close your eyes and concentrate on the year you wish to visit. It will only take you to the year, so whatever month and day you begin, that is where you will be in another era. Remember, you must focus with all your might on the year you wish to travel to. When you have reached your destination, do not lose this cloak as it is your only way back. When you are ready to return, do the process in reverse. If you choose to stay, after several weeks the cloak will return on its own to the present time. Good luck and Godspeed. And may all your dreams be fulfilled.

Lifting the cloak from its paper cocoon, Skye was disheartened. Certain she had been scammed, she clutched at the thing, but it slipped to the floor. Peering at it, it was unbelievably just a worn piece of fabric, complete with several moth holes. And it smelled musty. The cloth was so old it was not even identifiable.

A tear slipped down her cheek. All her savings, all her dreams and imaginings. Poof. Up in smoke. Just as she was about to get up and find out how good Ebay's return policy was, she noticed the cloak was warm to the touch. And vibrating. As if it contained something alive. As if it truly harbored power within its folds. Is this what magic felt like?

Unable to resist, she held a corner of it to her cheek and the buzzing sounds were unmistakable. Her mouth dropping open, she stood and reverently placed the garment back in its tissue paper and, smiling with all the faith in the world, went to her desk to make a list of the things she would need to take with her to Scotland.

Chapter Five

Pacing in front of the roaring fire, Ian was again lost in his dilemma.

Pushing back his long hair from his forehead, he mentally reviewed all his options. Fearing the lass in his visions was only a puff of smoke created by his tired mind, he had to face who was actually attainable. Freya was young and not too unpleasant to look at, but she was such a mouse as to be tiring. He didnae wish for a woman whose voice was grating and her demands many, but neither did he wish for one who would fade into the walls or the floor at the slightest provocation. Kenna was not so pleasing to the eye, but she was strong and capable and her skills in the kitchen well celebrated. That left Davina. It was well known she had used her wiles to acquire possessions, but it was at the cost of her reputation. Her endowments had tempted many, but he was not of a mind to be but one of many. And there was the lingering gossip that placed her in the center of many a misdeed. Unwilling to succumb to idle talk, he still had to wonder if there was any truth to the rumors.

Mayhap there was another from a neighboring clan that wished for an alliance that a wedding could encourage. But that was shaky ground at best. What if he met the woman they chose for him and he was less than happy? Not only would that not create friendly relations, it could start a war. Of course, marriages were not necessarily made out of mutual attraction. But he did wish for a wife he could make love to, instead of just bed out of obligation. Was that so much to ask? Frustration tightened his throat.

Dionadair, his small but fierce black terrier, sat near the fire, alert to every nuance of his master's moods. Laying down and dropping his head to his paws, he seemed to reflect Ian's predicament.

Stomping into the main room, Errol walked up to him. Handing Ian one of the mugs of ale he carried, he grinned.

"How goes your selection?" Errol's raised eyebrow only enhanced the smile quirking his lips.

Quaffing a huge swallow, Ian shook his head. "You hae an easy choice with my sister. She was the pick of the litter."

Errol's smile widened. "Aye and I came to share the news there will soon be another MacKenzie joining the fold."

Sharing his brother-in-law's joy, Ian clapped him on the back. "Well done."

"Shall we drink to it?"

They each took a hearty swig and found chairs next to the fire. "Mayhap you should be the laird," Ian suggested.

"Nay, you cannot escape your obligations so easily. I have no desire to have the headaches that come with those responsibilities. It is enough to tend the herds and see to my own."

"Then I need to marry." Ian said the words as if it was a sentence of death.

***

Sitting in a chair by the fire, Ian watched as Davina

sauntered over to him, a pitcher of ale in her hand. Pouring his horn full, she managed to nearly gag him with her proffered cleavage. Dionadair let out a short grumbling noise, his opinion of the woman clear.

"May I get you anything else, Laird? Anything at all? Something to ease the worry in yer brow?" Her seductive tone was too obvious to be enticing.

Angling forward, Davina appeared to stumble slightly, her hand landing on his thigh as her breasts nearly choked him. "Clumsy me." She giggled, then took her time straightening up.

Ian was unmoved by her awkward attempt at seduction and her pout was obvious as she stomped out of the hall.

His gaze moved to the crackling fire. It would be easy to wed her and bed her, but hell, she had made it clear she would be a willing partner, vows or no. And should she be fruitful and carry his heir, he could give the child a name. But he wanted more. He wanted a woman he could talk to, confide in, someone to counsel him and care about the clan more than herself. That woman was not Davina.

Staring into the flames, shapes took form, ephemeral and fleeting. It was as if there was a vision just out of his grasp. Something important he needed to know. "Then show yourself," he demanded.

Dionadair immediately perked up his ears and tilted his head, which elicited a chuckle from Ian. Absently, he reached out to stroke the dog's rough coat. "You know you fit your name. It means defender. Have I told you that?"

The dog gave a quick swipe of his tail, sending the rushes covering the floor in several directions.

"Brother?" his sister's voice interrupted.

Maisie sidled next to him, a curious frown marring her lovely face."Were you speaking to that dog again?"

"Well, he never disagrees with me." Smiling, he shook his head. "I was just lost in thought, mulling a problem. Naught for you to concern yourself." Looking closely at his sister, he could see the glow from the bairn she carried reflected in her cheeks. "I hear you are with child. That is welcome news."

Beaming, she lifted her shoulders and spun in a circle, her joy evident. Then, she sobered. "But it is time for you to father one of your own. With a wife."

Ian knotted his fists. "Not you, too. Does everyone in this clan have to remind me constantly of this need to marry and procreate? If I were nae to produce an heir, I am certain another could be found to follow after me."

Blinking as she took a step back in surprise at his reaction, she lowered her head. "Forgive me. I had no wish to upset you. I just want you to share this happiness."

Stricken, Ian stood and wrapped his arms around her. "No, forgive me. It has been a trying day and no fault of yours."

Releasing her, he smiled down at her. "I am much pleased to have another niece or nephew and soon enough, I will see he or she has a playmate."

Releasing her tension, Maisie smiled. "Is their aught I can do to help with your choices?"

"Nay. Unless you can conjure the perfect woman out of the air."

"That would be my hope. But I fear it will take magic, brother. You know I want naught more than your happiness. But my powers are somewhat limited."

***

50

The weather was turning colder, a portent of winter, but Ian had been soaked in sweat training the younger men fighting skills this morning. The afternoon had been spent settling minor disputes and supervising the building of new stables. By dusk, he was tired and hungry and in need of food and some ale.

The hall was filled with men and their conversation was interrupted by the clanswomen bringing in the trenchers for the evening meal. Ian made his way to the table with the others who had gathered. He had just sampled the savory fare when the hall door flew open amid a clattering of running feet.

"The queen was turned away from Inverness," Conall cried out as he raced into the great hall, several men at his heels. "And that devil, Alexander Gordon, slammed the door in her face. Orders from George Gordon, the sheriff of the county. And all of this to protect the son of the Earl and Countess of Huntly. The son, John, severely wounded Lord Ogilvie in a street brawl in Edinburgh as a result of which he was thrown into prison. But he escaped. Our queen wants their son in prison where he belongs, but they will not give him up." His eyes were wide with outrage.

Daimh lumbered to his feet, a arm in the air. "No one insults our queen or goes against her orders."

"We fight. Gather your weapons," Ian ordered. "No one dares to insult Queen Mary without retribution. I care not what office they hold." He pounded his fist on the table, causing the food and mugs of ale to leap. "We ride at first light."

***

The hour was late when Ian was finally able to make his way to his chamber for a few hours of sleep before dawn. The darkened room, lit only by the pale moonlight and the few flames that struggled to survive in the hearth, was awash in shadows. Dionadair trotted in behind him and was immediately on guard. His fur stood up on his back and his bared white teeth caught the light from the waning fire.

Instantly alert, Ian straightened, grabbed his dagger, prepared to deal with the intruder hiding under the furs.

In one swift motion, he pulled the coverings from the bed, his stance squared and ready. But instead of an enemy, Davina lay naked and clearly willing, a small smile on her face. Licking her lips, she motioned for him to join her. The dog growled again, and Ian shook his head.

"Get up and go to your own chamber. I am tired and need to rest before the journey on the morrow." He tried not to match the dog's snarl.

"I can give you pleasant memories for your trip," she replied.

Her attempt at seduction fell on deaf ears. "Davina, go. I appreciate your offering, but this is not the night."

Slowly, making certain he saw every inch of her nude body as she rose from the bed, she angled her way to the chair by the fire and reached for her cloak. Pouting in her obvious disappointment, she wrapped herself in the fabric and moved to the door. "When you return then?"

Following her to the door, he said "Goodnight, Davina," and firmly closed the portal behind her. Dionadair retreated to the bed and curled up at the foot, emitting a grumping noise as he settled. Ian nodded at him. "I tend to agree."

If the woman's flagrant display just now had not aroused him, he definitely needed to cross her name off his list for a possible wife.

Chapter Six

Skye was packing the last of her things into her case, her brain swirling with thoughts of everything before her. At first, she had pulled out a suitcase, but as she picked up the cloak, lovingly wrapped in the original tissue paper, she realized she dare not let it out of her sight. What if, heaven forbid, her suitcase was lost. Rummaging in her closet, she found on old leather carry-on. Examining the inside, she noticed the lining had come loose and she realized she could hide some of her modern necessities underneath. A needle and thread and it could be re-sewn, and no one would be the wiser if they looked into her case.

Carefully, she fit the cloak into the bag on top of the two gowns and the other garments. Along with underwear and two changes of regular clothes, she should have enough. It was a tight squeeze, but she had no choice.

Sinking onto the edge of her bed, she ticked off the list of toiletries she wanted to take, along with the antibiotics and insect repellent. Then she headed into her bathroom to retrieve a small deodorant crystal and a travel size body lotion. Realizing that wasn't a necessity, she put it back on the shelf. Transferring the deodorant into a small glass container, Skye decided she would do without the razor also. A bottle of aspirin, toothpaste, again transferred into a glass vial, and toothbrush. Obviously, she would have to hide these things, but she imagined it wouldn't be a problem. Or hoped it wouldn't be. Skye would miss many things about the twenty-first century, but it was a small price to pay for finding love and happiness.

All the items would work for the short term, but if she intended to stay, she'd have to follow their way of life, which would mean giving up a certain amount of hygiene.

Tucking the things into the corners of her bag for now, she checked off the tasks she had accomplished in the last few days, including haunting some antique stores for ancient British coins and getting an envelope with a customs form and postage so she could mail some things to Harper once she arrived in Scotland. She would need her phone and charger but didn't want to leave them behind when she traveled into the past.

She had spent hours studying the Scottish idioms, and word substitutions and refreshed her knowledge of the history of the area. *Would it be enough?*

Knocking interrupted her mental review. Inhaling deeply, knowing who it was, she strode to the front door and swung it wide.

Before Harper could speak, Skye held up her hand. "You're not going to talk me out of it," she stated firmly.

Harper slipped inside and walked over to the couch, slumping down into it. "I realize that. But I had to give it one more shot."

Skye sat down next to her and took hold of one of her hands. "I already know it's crazy. But I have to try. I'll never be satisfied otherwise."

"Have you really thought this through? I mean, what if the cloak actually works." The sarcasm was an obvious undertone. "Think about it. The fifteen hundreds? No indoor plumbing. No modern medicine. No regular baths. Or toilet paper." Harper shivered at this.

Leslie Hachtel

A giggle escaped Skye's lips. "Or tampons. And no makeup. But I am bringing a toothbrush, even though it wasn't invented until 1780." As if that was sufficient to sustain her. Harper clearly didn't see the humor.

"All your money. Your education. You're so close to your masters." Harper took hold of Skye's hands. "Please listen to reason. You know this is a dream, an impossibility,"

"School will still be there. And I will be able to experience history first-hand. What could be better?" Skye lifted her shoulders to make her point. "I can always work and make more money. I explained to the apartment owner I had a family emergency and he was very understanding. But he said if I wanted to keep my job, I had to be back in a week." Skye heaved a sigh. "I can't explain it. It's just something I have to do. And my stupid job will still be here if I fail."

Harper dropped her head in resignation. "When's your flight?"

"Tomorrow morning. And I can be at Eilean Donan Castle on the day of his return. I already booked a cottage for a week, and I have my backstory."

Harper raised an eyebrow and angled her head, silently urging Skye to continue with her fantasy. There was no doubt she was thinking she might find gaping holes in Skye's story and be able to discourage her.

"I was hoping to be part of Mary, Queen of Scots' court and was trying to join her at Inverness Castle when my guard and I were set upon. I managed to escape and made my way north and west. I ended up at Eilean Donan. My French is still more than passable and I'm hoping the Scots aren't fluent. My accent will certainly pass. And there you have it."

"Unbelievable," Harper scoffed. "I guess you've thought of everything. But, let me ask just one question."

"Go ahead," Skye responded, knowing she wouldn't like it.

"Will you call me and let me know what happens?"

Skye smiled. "If I don't, you will know I succeeded. I will text when I arrive. But if I do call you, stock your car with several bottles of wine when you pick me up at the airport." Skye took a deep breath and ran her hand through her hair. "If I don't call you, wait a week and come here, because it means it actually worked. The furniture stays, but take whatever else you want of mine. And don't forget me." A thought occurred. "Wait."

Skye ran over to the painting and reverently rolled it up. "Here," she said, handing it to Harper. "Take good care of this. No matter what happens, it changed my life."

"I will guard it with my life," Harper assured her, and there was no sarcasm in her tone. Wrapping Skye in a tight hug, Harper whispered. "You are the best friend I ever had, and I really do hope it all comes true. I really wish it was possible, for your sake. Even though I will miss you."

"Oh my God, I almost forget. How was your date?" Guilt at her self-involvement colored her words.

Harper's expression was downcast. "It was… nice. I don't think he's the man of my dreams and I don't even know if I want to see him again—but he did ask me."

"Yay! Nothing like a little black dress to get the job done. But…?"

"It was just so good to be with a man who actually listened to what I had to say. He didn't order food for me or tell me what I wanted to drink. And he told me I was beautiful."

"Again… but?"

"I don't know. I guess I want to be with someone who makes me feel safe. I know that sounds stupid since I'm fine on my own. It's just that… I think your ridiculous fantasies are rubbing off on me."

"Maybe they're not so ridiculous. Maybe when I get where I'm going, he can find a friend for you."

"I will miss you so much!" Harper wiped away a tear, made her way to the door, and slipped out.

***

For the thousandth time, Skye checked her passport and her wallet. Nervous energy flowed through her as she watched the frenzy of travelers, some walking by with determination, some checking the arrivals and departures board, and moving on. Their frenetic movements did nothing to help calm the adrenaline flowing through her.

Her flight would be called soon and the enormity of what she was doing was finally pressing down. Her breath hitching, she forced herself to relax and inhale slowly. *It's your Grand Adventure. It will be fine. And, added bonus, you might meet your soul mate. Soul mate. If that was a true thing, a soul wouldn't be bound merely by a few hundred years, right?*

"Flight 2012 to Edinburgh ready for boarding," came over the loudspeaker and Skye's hands shook so uncontrollably, she nearly dropped her boarding pass. "Go big or go home", she whispered under her breath, hugging her carry-on and putting one foot in front of the other.

***

Six and a half more hours on the train. Flushed with nerves and anticipation, Skye wiggled into her seat and re-read the information she had printed about Eilean Donan, even though every word was already committed to memory. It had been around since the early thirteenth century as a means of protection against the invading Vikings. Over the centuries, parts of it had been built up and torn down, but it still stood as master over the island and the surrounding lochs. And the pictures of the castle were breathtaking. Skye could only imagine what it would look like in real life.

The landscape sped by and a sense of peace eased into Skye's core. The world was so different here, so beautiful. Even civilization hadn't marred the gorgeous landscape, the hills covered in purple heather, the green so bright it almost hurt her eyes.

She had booked the cottage near the castle for seven nights. It cost more than the nearby apartments, but it was more private. The Ebay ad had even mentioned it: *Find the cottage lit by moonlight*. And she definitely wanted privacy. She hoped that three nights would be sufficient. Her heart would wither and her dreams would be crushed if this failed. There was that possibility, of course, but she banished it from her thoughts. Every mile was bringing her closer to the love of her life, her destiny. *Her destiny*. But she could not help but wonder what his name was.

***

1562

Perched on a hill and bathed in moonlight, Inverness Castle taunted the MacKenzies as they rode up below it.

The structure stretched across the landscape, the castellated towers boasting of strength. Built of red sandstone, it would not easily burn, but the men had prepared other means of attack. No one insulted their queen without paying the price.

On the ground below the rise, hundreds of men in various tartans moved about, their pent-up energy crackling in the damp September chill. The Munro, Ross, Fraser were all recognizable milling about. Any other time, these men would be at odds, but now they had a common goal.

Pleased to see so many other clans had risen to the occasion and quickly forgotten any petty feuds in favor of coming together to defend their queen, Ian smiled and ordered his men to dismount and tend the horses. Stepping across the field to the edge of a wooded area, Ian joined the other lairds gathered there.

A distance away, the royal tents glowed with torches, announcing Queen Mary would see this insult to its natural conclusion. She had faith in her fellow countrymen, knowing they would rise to the challenge of defending her. And so they had arrived with the intent of doing just that.

The men halted all motion and speech as the queen herself approached the group of leaders. Amber eyes that missed nothing swept her subjects and Ian was struck by her pale coloring, stark in the moonlight and swaying torchlight. Her confidence and the strength she exuded for a girl of but eighteen summers was indeed impressive. Ian surmised that widowhood at so young an age would have had that effect. Adversity either broke one or made one stronger.

The lairds bowed to her majesty, then laid out their

plan, which was a simple one. Inverness Castle was situated in a defensive position, but it depended more on its geography than actual fortifications. Word was there was not a sufficient garrison inside the walls and the castle itself was not properly prepared for sustaining an attack.

It was decided a battering ram would gain them access and men were immediately set to felling a huge tree and stripping its branches for the purpose. The Frasers and Munros would lead the charge as they pressed through the gates. Their targes, inch-thick shields held over their heads, would protect them from fire or even boiling oil dropped from above. The shields were sturdy enough, with their studded leather front and fur backing, to withstand most any assault. Convinced that once inside they would face no serious challenge, they decided to attack at first light.

Pleased, the queen retired to her tent. In the morning, she would call for the attack and await the outcome, having made it clear she intended to spend nights in the castle as soon as it was secured.

Ian was happy to bask in the camaraderie as they broke bread and exchanged news of the English encroachment and the heinous crimes of their neighbors to the South. Most of Scotland was united in two things: hatred of the English and love of their queen.

By the time pink and orange edged the bottom of the sky, the men were ready. Mary sounded the charge and the men surged forward. The hammering of the ram rattled the castle gates and resonated through the countryside. Soon, it was the clash of metal that replaced the pounding and, after three days of brutal combat, the castle fell to the onslaught of the clans.

Chapter Seven

The cottage was lovely. Even better than the pictures. She paid the driver who had brought her from the train station and just inhaled. Scotland was, in itself, like a fairy tale. The greens were vibrant, the scent in the air flavored with what had to be the end of the season heather, and the very ground throbbed with history and promise. The cold air was bracing and fueled the rush of blood in her veins. And over there, across the stone bridge, the castle beckoned. The stone bridge. That was the first thing she would look for in the morning.

Over the centuries, the castle had expanded and contracted in size. Smaller now, in 1562 it had probably dominated the entire island, but today it looked as ancient as the world in which it had been built.

The loch glowed beneath the rays of sun streaming through the clouds, reflecting the structure it surrounded. It dared any miscreant to cross over. Behind, the dark mountains rose creating a spectacular vision.

The familiarity of it all stunned her, as if she had been here before. Not just in the pictures. It was welcoming, like coming home.

Tempted to run across the bridge to the castle, she resisted. No, she decided. She would be patient until tomorrow. If she made the trip through time, it would only be disconcerting in the changes over the centuries. And, if for some unthinkable reason she did not travel across the years, she would have days to explore the place before she had to return home.

"Soon," she whispered, as she let herself inside the cottage, clutching her bag and all that it promised. "I will know my fate soon."

Inside, the space was warm and elegant. Two bedrooms, each with its own beautifully equipped bathroom. Large airy windows with a one hundred eighty-degree panoramic view of the surrounding Lochs. The heavy oak furniture was covered in lavish fabrics and tweeds.

In front of one of the windows, a small writing desk complete with stationery and a pen with a feather quill spoke of times when people actually wrote letters to each other. Squatting in the corner, a wood burning fireplace waited, filled with kindling and a log, a welcome sight in the chilled room.

Skye wasn't accustomed to such lavish accommodations, but it would be easy enough to get used to living in places like this. And no one would be knocking on her door to demand she repair a broken pipe or ask why the refrigerator was humming so loud.

It was only midday and Skye was exhausted, but her thoughts were way too energized to even consider sleep. She realized she was starving, though, and the driver had told her of several places in the nearby village to enjoy a good meal. Anxious to sightsee while she still could, she made her way to the door, then looked back at the carry-on she had dropped by the couch. Even now, she dared not leave it behind. She grabbed her bag and the keys she had left by the door, then made her way down to the shops. The village was glorious, the true definition of picturesque. Small shops crowded together in comfortable co-existence. She took a few pictures to send to Harper and let her know she had arrived safely.

Something delicious wafted on the breeze just as Skye found herself in front of Clachan Pub. Her stomach growled reminding her she hadn't eaten in hours. And so she ducked inside to sample the local fare.

Just as she had imagined, the place was cozy and warm. Wood walls and floor, a bar that dominated the back wall with bottles of all kinds glittering in the sparse light, and a welcoming hostess who smiled broadly as she led Skye to a table in the corner made her want to hug herself with joy.

"American?" she asked, her Scottish brogue thick.

"How could you tell?" Skye responded, almost fearful of the woman's answer.

"Well, I know the locals, and this is the season for tourists." She handed Skye a menu. "I'd love to see your country someday. Is American as vast and wonderful as they say?"

"Yours is so beautiful, I can't imagine wanting to ever leave."

The woman nodded. "Aye, t'is a lovely place. But I do yearn to see more of the world someday. Can I get you some ale?"

Skye grinned. "Absolutely. Whatever you recommend." A thought occurred. "Can you make that a whiskey instead?"

The woman nodded and a few minutes later, a short glass with dark brown liquid was set before her. Ordering fish and chips, her mouth watered in anticipation. Tentatively, she lifted the glass of whiskey and inhaled the aroma of smoke and peat, then sipped. It burned a pleasant, heated path to her stomach and Skye relaxed. She was here, walking the same ground he had walked. Scotch would have been new in 1562, called usquebaugh or aquavitae, which translated to water of life, although alcohol in the form of ale was more common.

Skye realized this was already a Grand Adventure, no matter the outcome. What she was experiencing now was exciting, so different from her everyday life in Memphis. It was worth every dime, even if this was all there was. But she quickly banished that thought. Tomorrow she would be meeting the man of her dreams. She had to hold onto that thought.

After a delicious meal, Skye poked about the shops and inhaled the sweet air. This was a wonderful place, even if the cloak failed her. If she was still here the next day, it would be a consolation prize. Hating the idea that the cloak might not work, she nevertheless knew it was a possibility. But she needed to keep her faith strong, at least until the morning, since tonight was the night that would determine her future.

***

When she returned to her cottage, Skye sat down at the desk. Taking her passport, driver's license, and some of her cash and tucking them into the envelope she had brought with her, she addressed it to Harper. Picking up a piece of stationery, she wrote a note to go with the items.

> *Harper-*
> *You have been my best friend for as long as I can remember. I know you think this is all crazy, but if you are getting this note, the cloak*

worked and I am off to find my one true love. As the line goes from "The Wizard of Oz"—I will miss you most of all.

Be happy for me and I hope you find the man of your dreams. Remember, don't settle for the first one to come along. You are the best—never forget that and hold out for someone wonderful.

With love,

Your BFF, (and in this case, forever is more than 450 years)

Skye

Sealing the note inside, she placed stamps on the envelope along with the customs form and hoped whoever found it would send it on. She thought of mailing it herself, but if the cloak turned out to be a disappointment, she would need those things to return home.

Later, curling up on the couch with a brochure of local attractions, her eyelids drooping, Skye knew the time had come. A tingle of fear tracked up her spine, but she straightened her back and, grabbing her case, she strode into the bedroom.

Knowing she would not get regular baths from now on, she took a leisurely shower, taking care to scrub off any remnants of the little makeup she usually wore, and wrapped up in the fluffy robe thoughtfully provided. After brushing her teeth, she tucked the aspirin, antibiotic, toothbrush and toothpaste, and deodorant into the space between the lining and the leather of her case.

She separated the modern clothes from the bag and folded them on top of the bureau along with her underwear. Sitting cross-legged on the bed, she pulled out the sewing kit and, careful to take small nearly invisible stitches, closed the gap in the lining of her bag. Lastly, squeezing her phone, she turned it off and, along with the charger, placed it on the dresser next to her modern clothes. There was something very final about that, but Skye was pretty certain she wouldn't be able to get any cell service where she was going. *Where she was going? Was it possible?* Then, she scribbled a quick note to the owner of the cottage.

Thank you for a lovely visit. I had to leave suddenly, so I am hoping you will send these things on to my friend Harper. Her address is on the other envelope. I hope this money will cover any costs. Thank you again for everything. Skye Blaine.

Laying the remaining cash on top, she inhaled and mentally prepared for her new, hundreds-year-older self. Stepping into the red velvet gown, she tightened the laces, then arranged her curls on top of her head. There was a moment of panic as she realized she had no decoration for her hair. But she calmed herself, she could always say it was lost. She decided against the wide collar, thinking it too awkward to sleep in and she could always say she lost it as well. It, too, was placed on the chest. The thought of someone discovering all these things made her laugh. What would they think?

A long look in the bathroom mirror convinced her she looked good enough to pass. She hoped.

And suddenly, it was no longer a game, a fantasy. This was real. She was in Scotland, away from all she held familiar, waiting to be transported back in time. Involuntarily, her body quivered with a combination of excitement, anticipation, and sheer terror. What if it worked? What if it didn't?

Skye took a deep breath. She had come this far. What was the worst that could happen? She would wake up in this charming place, explore and shop. Her dreams would evaporate, but this reality was not so bad. It was beautiful here, and historical.

"No!" she said out loud. "I have to try. I can make back the money, I can get my job back, I can go back to school." Those thoughts filled her with a terrible ache, but she was nothing if not a realist. She would put on the cloak and she would have faith. Above all, she would trust until she could no longer maintain her belief in… magic.

Then, reverently lifting the cloak, she placed her bag on the bed, enfolded it in her arms, and wrapped herself tightly in the fabric.

A moment of doubt caused her forehead to crease. *Am I being ludicrous? Seriously, time travel? Skye, you have to grow up and leave the fairy tales of your childhood behind. There is no magic. This cloak smells and I've wasted all my money and what is wrong with me?*

Inhaling deeply, determination kicked doubt aside. What was done was done and it wouldn't hurt to at least give this a shot.

"1562, 1562, 1562…"

***

What was that smell? It was even worse than the cloak. *And why is it so cold?*

The strangest dreams had invaded her rest. She had been in what felt like a wind tunnel, the rush of air hot and frigid at the same time. Climbing, her knees shaking

68

as if they would not support her for long, she saw light streaming into the darkness, but the rush of air sucked at her breath and pressed down on her chest. And then calm. Absolute stillness except for the trilling of a bird in the distance. And a throbbing headache.

Skye blinked back sleep as awareness crept in. Securely wrapped in the cloak, a different chill feathered its way under the fabric, bringing her to full wakefulness. Sitting up so quickly dizziness clouded her vision, Skye couldn't believe what she was seeing. She threw the cloak aside and looked around the small room. Her head pulsed in a painful rhythm and her heart pounded so hard it hurt her ribs.

Did it really work? Or was she still dreaming?

The cozy, richly decorated cottage was now a crumbling combination of old timbers and damp straw. The soft mattress was a lumpy mass of God knew what and it was so cold. The mattress itself was huddled on the floor without a bed frame. No welcoming fireplace danced with warmth and... the smell. Wet animal. It is so cold, she repeated to herself.

Oh my God, it *did* work! It was real! Adrenaline flooded through her like lightning. Gulping air, she inhaled, only slightly calming her racing heart. The thought repeated—was she in 1562? Really? Or was she still asleep? Maybe this was just a very real dream. Suddenly, terror gripped her. What had she done? Puffing air through dry lips, she reminded herself that if the cloak worked to bring her here, it could as easily take her back. That's what the note had read. Slightly reassured and still caught up in disbelief, she blinked and moved to the edge of the mattress.

Standing slowly, her arms stiff from clutching her

bag, Skye released the thing, placing it to the side. She then took a few tentative steps to what had once been a door but was now a crooked plank hanging from what appeared to be leather hinges. Peering out, the surface of the loch twinkled in the early morning light, blues and pinks and oranges reflecting off its glistening surface. Fog, no doubt dense earlier, was lifting, giving an ethereal quality to the landscape. And in the distance in front of her, looking as if it dared her to question its existence, was Eilean Donan castle rising like an imaginary vision. The structure occupied the same space as it had yesterday, but there were things about the scene that definitely suggested differences. The loch was still there, the majestic mountains rising in the distance, but the building itself was larger and the stones brighter, newer, although they still wore the stains of age and weather.

The screeching of a bird flying low caught her attention and she looked up. Fog still obscured the sky, and a breeze washed her cheek. Just as it had… hundreds of years ago yesterday?

And then it struck her like a dash of cold water: the bridge to the castle was gone. The castle now sat regally on an island with no direct access, unlike the castle she had seen the night before. Instead, wooden boats of various sizes rocked in the early morning sway of the water. Remembering the bridge hadn't been built until the reconstruction of the castle in 1919, her mouth dropped open. The professor had told her, and she could now see for herself.

Stepping out a little further and peering down the road, the pub where she'd had dinner the night before was no longer visible. Only some cottages in various states of disrepair were evident. And there was a village, although it was nothing like the one she had seen just—yesterday. There were some small shops, but they were comparatively primitive. In the distance, people were milling around wearing the strange dress of medieval times.

Again, she turned to the castle to re-affirm the bridge had disappeared and was not just masked by the shimmering sun or some other optical illusion. Squinting, and turning her head, then moving right and left, it was clear. No bridge.

Stepping back inside to the mattress, she reached for the cloak, reverently folded it, and put it back into her case. Shivering, she nevertheless worried that if the cloak had indeed worked its magic, she might as easily be transported back if she put it back on for warmth. If this were all real, that is. But, she had to make certain she didn't lose sight of it. It was her only way back.

Approaching the opening again, and walking outside, the mooing of cows and the bleating of sheep nearby cut through the morning quiet. Off to her left, an older woman was shooing some goats into a pen and Skye stepped back into the darkness of the cottage, but not before the woman spotted her and, hands on hips, strode over in her direction.

Her gray hair covered by a dirty scarf, the other woman looked every bit of sixty but, if this was truly 1562, she was probably closer to half that age. There was something so familiar about her. Mrs. Baggins! She looked just like Mrs. Baggins. Only clothed in a long skirt and blouse with a vest of sorts. Was that even possible? No, this had to be a dream. Pinching herself, Skye was still unconvinced of the reality here, even though she so wanted to believe.

"My lady?" The question summed up her confusion

at seeing Skye emerging from the ruined structure. Her brogue was thick.

"Bonjour," Skye responded, her veins pulsing with excitement. It was like the curtain rising on a fabulous play.

The other woman cocked her head and squinted. "French?"

"Oui, madam," Skye smiled.

"How do you come here?" she asked, angling her head in confusion. "Do you speak English?"

Skye took a deep breath. "I do. Where is here?" She feigned ignorance, thinking it the best idea.

"Why, you're in Dornie. There…" she pointed to the castle, "is Eilean Donan Castle." The last was said with pride.

Although she had to bite her tongue, Skye dared not ask the year or be thought slow witted. Instead, she launched into her carefully prepared rhetoric, concentrating on her French accent. "I was set upon. I was trying to meet my queen at Inverness Castle when my guards and I were attacked. I managed to escape and rode until my horse gave out. And walked more until I saw this cottage. It was so dark and I was so tired. I only meant to rest for a bit." She heaved a breath for emphasis. "I don't know where I am or how to return and I fear for my men."

"Your queen? Mary, of Scots?"

"Oui. I am hoping to be with her court."

That evoked a nod and a smile, revealing broken yellow teeth. "Oh, you pur dear. My name is Neasa and I serve the laird. We all do. He is gone to rescue the queen in Inverness but should return soon. Bide here at the castle and he will see to your return."

"Rescue the queen?" Skye managed to sound

horrified. "Who would dare threaten her?" Of course, Skye knew perfectly well he'd gone to Inverness Castle with the other clans. The man in the portrait was certainly with the laird. Or, perhaps, he *was* the laird. Which would make sense, since mere clansmen did not have their portraits painted.

Neasa smiled more broadly now, the lines in her face deepening. "Ye need not be feart. Laird Ian does not lose in battle. The queen will be safe." Her smile was confident. "I was just tending the goats, but I'm ready to return, so come with me and I shall see ye cared for. Huv ye eaten?"

Skye shook her head, grateful to be taken under the wing of this sweet woman who definitely reminded her of Mrs. Baggins. And the older woman had said she was a MacKenzie. Oh my God, this was becoming more and more real. What would Harper say if she could see Skye now?

"I just need my things," she explained, hurrying back into the old hut to retrieve her bag. She pinched herself again and the sharp pain on her arm was almost enough to convince her this was no hallucination.

Returning to Neasa, Skye followed her slowly, her head shifting from side to side to continually reassure herself that what she was seeing was real. Or rather, the things she was not seeing. There was no sign of civilization as she knew it.

The smell of Scotland was so much more intense now, without the vestiges of civilization. The air was bracingly cold, sweet, and almost painfully sharp. Sage and earth and the remnants of smoke.

Neasa led her to a wooden boat large enough for two. It struck Skye that the craft was rickety at best and was grateful she could swim. As Neasa paddled closer to

73

the castle, Skye's cheeks flushed, and her heart thudded to a staccato beat. The older woman rowed with practiced movements until they soon reached a jetty that abutted the rocks below the structure. Neasa tied off the craft and jumped up onto the dry land. "Follow me," she said, smiling.

The lingering sense of unreality held her in its grip, but its grasp was loosening. Her gaze traveled upward. The towering structure was breathtaking, even more so than when she had seen it from a distance the day before. She was here and people actually lived and worked within its walls.

Skye followed Neasa up a path to the building, through the gates, and across the courtyard. It was like entering a Renaissance faire. People bustled about dressed in period clothing, the clanging of a blacksmith struck a steady rhythm in the distance, and everyone seemed to be occupied with one task or another. A few of the women stopped at their chores to stare, but Skye noticed Neasa's quelling looks and they returned to their labors.

This was history alive. Not like reading about it. It was almost too much to take in. Hoping this wasn't all just a figment of her imagination, Skye embraced every part of this experience. There was still that kernel of doubt. Maybe she was still asleep?

One woman strode up, hips swaying, arms akimbo. Narrowing her eyes, she glared at Skye. "And who is this?"

The woman was taller than Skye, appeared to be about her age, with her ample bust well displayed. She was pretty in a tight sort of way, her eyes without sparkle and her lips pinched. Her glare was less than warm.

Neasa didn't bother to muffle an exaggerated sigh. "This is…" She looked at Skye. "I didnae get your name."

"I am Skye. Skye Blaine." Luckily her last name was a combination of Gaelic and Scottish.

Neasa nodded and turned back to the other woman. "Davina, this pur gurl was set upon and barely escaped with her life. She is a lady-in-waiting to our queen."

"Then what does she here?" To say sympathy was lacking was a huge understatement.

Neasa rolled her eyes. "I just explained. She was on her way to join Queen Mary when her party was attacked. And now I am going to get her some food."

"What do ye hold onto so tightly?" Davina asked, indicating Skye's bag, and making her question sound more like an accusation.

"All I could save. Some clothes, a few keepsakes." *Lotion, deodorant, a bottle of aspirin, some antibiotics. Oh, yes, and a magic cloak. Things that would get me branded as a witch.*

Skye could not restrain a small grin as Neasa pushed past Davina, pulling Skye along by her arm. Neasa shook her head. "She's a bit crabbit unless Ian is here. And one as comely as yourself she will only view as a threat. But the others will welcome you, fear not."

"Ian?" Skye asked.

"Our laird. He is without a wife to give him an heir and Davina has her sights on the task. Not that to be his wife would be a hardship for any wummin." Neasa raised her eyebrows. "You'd not be betrothed, my lady?"

Ian. The laird's name was Ian. Ian MacKenzie. Was he the man in the painting? Somehow she knew the answer.

75

Neasa's words registered. "Betrothed? Non. I am not."

Neasa responded with an ear-to-ear grin.

The huge carved wooden doors to the main hall were open and Skye gasped as they entered. Stone walls rose to thick crossbeams and an enormous fireplace lit the room with dancing flames. The walls themselves were covered in faded tapestries and her skirt whispered across the rushes covering the floors. It was like being on a movie set, only so much more. Just like the descriptions of historical places she had read about. Her eyes had widened as wide as saucers, but she couldn't help herself. Living history. Amazing.

Knowing the Scots were a frugal people, she had not expected the incredibly beautiful wood carvings everywhere: on the furniture, the doors, the thresholds. Paintings decorated some of the walls and—there—hanging near the stone steps, was *the portrait* that had brought her here. Stifling a gasp and staring, it took an effort of will to pull her gaze from the picture she knew so well. If nothing else convinced her of where she was, seeing the painting brought reality home.

Neasa noticed Skye had stopped and was staring at the portrait.

"'Tis a fine likeness of the laird. Conall is most talented. He be the one who painted him. Captured the laird to the life."

So the man she had come to find was the laird. Her instincts had been right. Laird Ian. Her heart beat in her throat as she imagined actually meeting him.

Neasa continued to walk through the main area, down a wide corridor, and into the kitchen. Recovering herself, Skye quickly followed. Skye was directed to a small rough-hewn table with attached bench seats off to the side and she sat. Grabbing a bowl, and filling it with a thick porridge, Neasa added honey and milk, and a piece of oat cake, then placed it in front of Skye.

"I hae no doubt you be used to better, but the men should be returning soon, and they will want food and ale in the hall."

"It looks wonderful. Merci."

Spooning the delicious warm food into her mouth, Skye listened to Neasa explain who was who and what they did at the castle. Skye was delighted she didn't have to say much or ask too many questions. The shock of travelling to 1562 was wearing off and she desperately wanted to meet the laird, since she was certain he was the man in the portrait. And he was unmarried. Her heart gave a little thrill at that.

Chapter Eight

The conflict had taken three days. The stench of spilled blood permeated the landscape, the warmth of the late summer sun making the smell worse as the defeated gathered their dead and carted them off for burial.

Alexander Gordon, he who had shut the castle gates in the face of his queen, swayed lifeless from the new gallows, the rope around his neck creaking mournfully in the errant breeze. Labeled a traitor, he would be buried in an unmarked grave and his head would be displayed on the castle walls for all to see. The small number of able Gordon supporters who had survived, numbering less than fifteen, were sequestered in the dungeons below the castle, but the defenders of the queen showed mercy to the innocent people of the village and allowed them to be set free.

Triumphant, the queen waited until the carnage had been cleared, then swept into the castle and had the largest bedroom prepared. As she had promised, she planned to sleep within these walls for four nights before moving on to Spynie Palace, where she would be welcomed.

Exhausted, dirty, and filled with victory, Ian and his men made their way back home. It was five days more until their castle finally came into view across the loch. The men kicked their horses forward, eager for rest and good food.

Dismounting and passing their tired horses off to the waiting grooms, the soldiers clamored into the waiting boats and rowed home.

Spirits high, they strode into the main hall and took their places at the benches set in the middle of the space. The tables were immediately laden with trenchers filled with meat, bread, and cheese and cups nearly overflowed with ale. The room fell silent as the men ate and then, refreshed, the clamor began. Those left behind were anxious to hear every detail of the battle and the defense of their queen. When it was announced the villain had been hanged, a cheer rang out.

***

Inside the kitchen, the sudden noise jolted Skye and she stood and grabbed her bag. No matter what, she dare not let it out of her sight. Creeping closer to the main hall, a push from behind, courtesy of Neasa, and she was suddenly next to where the laird sat, drinking ale.

The movement caught his attention and he turned to face her. Skye inhaled sharply. Here he was, in the flesh. Her mouth went dry and her blood pounded in her ears. Her knees didn't actually seem to be supporting her, and she wondered how she was still standing. Neasa offered a happy distraction by stepping forward.

"Laird, welcome home. This is the Lady Skye."

His gaze was piercing, and he was magnificent. She'd never experienced a painting come to life, but in the flesh he was so much—better. Angling his head, he gave her the oddest look. A smile lifted his lips and he blinked, as if he thought she might not be real. Odd. Skye was the one with the utter and complete sense of unreality.

Standing there and staring at him, Skye remained stunned. It was him. Living, breathing, in front of her, filling her vision. His hair was brighter than in the portrait and his eyes—she had been right. They were the blue of the gemstones. Broad shoulders and muscular arms were visible beneath his linen shirt. And those legs. Muscular calves rose to a brief glimpse of powerful thighs, and she knew that above those, no underwear bound his manhood. He was mesmerizing.

Skye had never fainted before in her life, so she was unaware what it meant when everything flashed white and her traitorous knees buckled. Strong arms grabbed her before she fell, steadying her, as she caught her breath. The arms supporting her were like steel and she was pressed against a chest of solid muscles. Was this all her imagination? No man could look like this, feel like this.

Frozen, she dared not speak, fearing he would disappear like smoke. Or *she* might. He lifted her as he stood and smiled again. Her insides melted. He dropped his head in an abbreviated bow. "My lady. Are you unwell?"

More handsome than the picture, more appealing, more... he took her breath away. And that brogue, the way the tartan exposed his knees, the sporran—all of it— all of him was almost too much to bear.

"I... I'm fine. Sorry. Just... tired?" Her response seemed ludicrous to her.

"She hae been through an ordeal, laird," Neasa offered.

Luckily, a snuffling at her feet broke through, garnering her attention and she leaned down. Big brown eyes in a black furry face stared back at her, then whooshed its tail, disturbing the rushes.

"Dionadair approves." Ian laughed, shaking his

head in almost a question. This was clearly not a common occurrence. "He is generally not very fond of wummin."

"Your dog is so handsome," Skye said, and the dog appeared to understand, since his hind end moved more furiously.

"And whence came you, my lady?" Ian asked, lifting her back to standing, and leading her to the table.

Easing next to him on the bench, her pulse fluttering, she pressed her lips together and inhaled. Tucking her bag between her ankles, it offered a measure of comfort.

Skye straightened her spine and repeated the story she had told Neasa, working to maintain her French accent, and hoping it was convincing.

"And your men?" he asked.

"I fear them dead. They told me to flee, and I did. It was cowardly."

Reaching out, he touched her shoulder. A spark of electricity jolted her. Unwilling to give away her attraction to the man, she leaned over again to pet the pup, who now sat next her feet and preened under her touch.

Moving closer to her, Skye inhaled the scent of man and horse and woodsmoke and... man.

"Oh no, my lady. You speak like our queen. But a battle is never a place for a lady, especially one of your sensibilities." He gestured to the seat next to him. "Please, tell me more of your adventures."

"I would much more like to hear of how you saved our queen, Laird."

"I am Ian."

Skye could feel the blush warm her cheeks at his scrutiny and another, clearly hostile glare from the woman, Davina, who stood behind the laird with a ready pitcher of ale. *So Neasa was right. She has her sights on him.* After living with her mother, Skye knew a threat when she saw it. She would have to be cautious around this woman.

Ian reached across the table and placed a trencher in front of Skye and served her some meat with leeks and garlic.

"Eat. It will strengthen you," he said, and the only thought in her head was she wanted to crawl into his lap and hold tight.

Unwilling to be rude by telling him she had just eaten, she picked at the food. Ian recounted the battle again and Skye managed to look both shocked and surprised, although she knew all about what had transpired. Sitting next to him, the warmth of his body seeping into her soul, Skye still could not fathom the certainty of all this. The timbre of his voice was deep and seductive, and Skye was mesmerized. She reined in her instinct to touch him and focused on his words.

At one point her shoulder brushed his arm and all she could think of was... wow. She had read about the almost electric shock that passed between lovers, but it was a totally new experience. He had startled at the contact. Did he feel it, too?

Trying to control herself and resist staring at the face she had studied for weeks, she found she could not completely pull her gaze from him, so she watched his hands, his chest as he inhaled, his shoulders as he leaned in to her. Controlling her breathing was an act of sheer will. When she met his gaze with her own, their blue depths nearly drowned her, so she kept her eyes averted as much as possible.

"And tell me of your life with our queen?" Ian prodded.

"Well, as I said, I have not actually spent time with her majesty. I always wanted to serve as one of her ladies. My mother was French nobility, you see, and my father was Scottish. I was preparing to depart for court when word came Queen Mary had been widowed and decided to return home to Scotland. My mother and father thought it a perfect opportunity to follow Queen Mary to this country and serve her. Before I could depart, my parents contracted a terrible sickness. When they succumbed, I decided to follow their wishes, to leave France and go to the Scottish court to serve. Our queen is strong and will always prevail and it would honor me to be part of her retinue. Especially since she is now without her husband. And at such a young age."

How well she knew of the fate of Mary of Scotland and all the bad choices she made before it ended in her beheading. Skye sniffed. "Besides, I had no one left in France and nowhere else to go. I was actually born in Scotland." The concocted tale slipped easily from her lips.

"She must have received word of the attack on you and your men by now. I shall send a messenger to Spynie Palace to ease her mind that you are safe."

Panic gripped her. If Mary received such a message, Skye would no doubt be exposed. "Oh, no, Laird…"

"Ian."

"Ian. Please do not fash yourself." *She had watched Outlander. That's what Jamie said all the time to Claire. Would it make her sound Scottish, too, since she was trying to convince them of her roots here?* "I will write to my queen, but give her time to recover. The insult at Inverness must have been distressing for her and I doubt she will hear about my fate for some time, if at all. As I

83

said, I followed her here to Scotland to petition to serve her. Being of noble birth, I hoped she would accept me. I can send my appeal when she has had time to get over the terrible offense she has just suffered."

"You have a kind heart," he said, his voice low and warm, which elicited another death glare from Davina. "Well, then, you shall stay with us until you receive an answer. And then, of course, when the time comes, my men will escort you."

Davina leaned closer, pressing her bosom against Ian's shoulder, and leaving little to the imagination. "But, Laird, wouldn't the lady be more comfortable if she was on her way sooner rather than later. No doubt the Queen could use more ladies to comfort her."

Forcing her expression to remain neutral, Skye responded. "I thank you, Davina, but it would be good to take a short time to rest before beginning my journey anew. And no doubt, the laird's men must be tired after their... brave adventure." Giving Ian her broadest smile, she was gratified when he returned it and nodded agreement.

"So it is settled." He turned his head. "Neasa," he called out. The older woman was immediately at his side.

"Laird?"

"Please show the Lady Skye to a chamber so she may rest after her ordeal."

Feeling his eyes on her as she followed Neasa up the stone steps, she remembered to straighten her posture and move with the grace of a lady. What she really wished was to turn back and throw herself into his arms, but she knew better. This had to be destiny and her opportunity would come.

***

The pup was actually following her. Dionadair was notoriously a woman-hater and his loyalty to his master was unquestionable. And yet, here he was, leaving Ian's side and trailing behind the most appealing woman Ian had ever laid eyes upon. *Mayhap he recognizes her, too.*

When Ian first saw her, something opened inside him. It was as if he had waited all his life for her to appear. At the same time, it was as if he had known her for an eternity. It wasn't just that she was fair of face or had a body any man would ache to hold. There was something about the way she looked at him that made him feel as if he could conquer anything. That was it. That feeling. That was why she was so familiar, although in truth, he had never seen her face in his dreams. But this was the one who had filled his nights.

"She is *Francach*" his brother-in-law whispered. "Ye swore you would never marry either a Frenchwoman or a *Sassenach*."

Ian turned on Errol with a look of feigned outrage. He had no intention of letting on how this woman was affecting him. "Who said anything about marry? I just met the woman."

Errol grinned and raised an eyebrow. "Then you should wipe the drool from the side of your mouth. Quite unbecoming to a laird."

Returning Errol's smile, Ian shook his head. "It's that blasted dog. Seems he forgets where his loyalties lay."

"You mean the dog that hates wummin? Or is he feeding off his master?"

"You're enjoying yourself," Ian snapped.

"I am," Errol agreed. "'Tis a new experience to see both you and the dog so disarmed."

"She is—lovely."

"You'll need the queen's permission. Since she's one of her ladies."

Ian snorted. "Dae you not think you're rushing this? And besides, you heard her. She is not one of the Queen's court as yet."

Errol snorted and moved to his wife, then whispered in her ear. She stared at her brother, her mouth open, laughed and clapped her hands.

Ian sank into his chair and quaffed the remaining ale in his mug, his thoughts swirling. Yes, he had sworn to only marry a Scotswoman, but it wasn't a true vow, was it? It was then he remembered she had said she was born in Scotland and her father was Scottish. So, she wasn't truly French. Her surname was actually Scots.

He could only wonder at his turn of thought. Until a few hours ago, he had thought of marriage as a torture he needed to endure, a necessary distraction he could nae afford. But seeing the Lady Skye—imagining the softness of her flesh, the taste of those perfect pink lips—and he was re-thinking all he had conjured about taking the dreaded vows of matrimony. And she did not ask for favors or offer herself freely. Her interest in him seemed sincere. And those green eyes—well, he could gaze into them forever. Would it be so terrible to marry a woman not of his clan? Skye was young and beautiful and could no doubt produce heirs.

"Laird?" Daimh's deep voice interrupted, and Ian immediately turned to his friend.

"Aye?"

"You need to have a blether with two of the farriers. There's another dispute aboot their tools."

Surreptitiously glancing at the stone steps leading to the upstairs chambers, Ian stood and followed Daimh into the courtyard.

***

Opening a door at the end of a corridor at the top of the stairs, Neasa stepped aside and ushered Skye into a bed chamber. It was much larger than her entire apartment back home. The walls were lined with fabric, the material was old and threadbare, but had clearly once been beautiful. The room itself was clean, with fresh rushes on the floor and a huge fireplace off to the left. But the bed was the centerpiece. It was huge, with carved wooden head and foot boards. Four columns supported the upper panel, from which drapes provided both privacy and kept in the warmth. At the foot, a large, dark wood chest bound with iron squatted importantly. The dog ran to the bed and jumped up, claiming his place, and Skye couldn't help but smile. She hadn't had a pet since hers was sent away when she was a child, and the prospect of having a warm, furry companion through the night was appealing.

Neasa stared at the pup and her eyebrows came together in obvious confusion. "Dionadair hae never done such a thing."

Looking to Neasa for an explanation, the older woman laughed. "He never sleeps anywhere but the laird's chamber. In fact, he has ne'er followed a female except to growl." Neasa smiled. "Mayhap it is an omen."

Skye understood her meaning and silently hoped that was the case.

"The garderobe is behind that alcove." Neasa pointed to the far-right corner of the room. "It is none too fancy, as I have nae doubt you are used to the furnishings at the French court, but it should suit your needs."

Skye spun around to Neasa and wrapped her in a hug. The other woman resisted for a moment, then hugged back. "You have been so kind to me."

Neasa stepped away and smoothed her skirt, her embarrassment clear. Apparently ladies did not hug staff, or whatever they were called here.

Neasa cleared her throat. "We are honored to have you here. And hope you plan to stay for a while. We could use the guidance of one who knows so much of the world."

"I suppose there is no real rush to get to the court now that the queen is safe. Thanks to your clansmen." The Battle of Corrichie was coming on October 28th. She would rather be here than in Aberdeen with the Queen. But the thought of Ian fighting terrified her. Even though she knew he would not be killed. No one from his group would be harmed in the fight. It was reassuring to know the facts, but it didn't lessen the underlying worry.

"Rest now. The evening meal will be ready in a few hours."

"Thank you so much, Neasa. But would it be all right if I went for a short walk? I would love to explore the castle and grounds."

Anxious to take in every aspect of this adventure, Skye had no desire to sleep. In fact, sleep worried her, especially if this was only a dream that would dissipate when she woke up.

"You can do whatever you please. You must consider this your home as long as you bide with us. I must see to the kitchen, but if you need anything, just let one of the women know."

And she swept from the room.

Still clutching her bag and reluctant to release it, Skye knew she had to put it somewhere. The chest would be perfect, and she reasoned that anyone looking at it wouldn't know to rip away the lining and expose her secrets. Nor would anyone realize the power of the cloak without wrapping themselves in it.

Lifting the heavy lid, she saw several lovely gowns carefully folded inside. Lifting one and holding it up, it obviously belonged to someone of means. The embroidery around the collar and cuffs was done with the tiniest of stitches, depicting flowers and leaves. It put Skye's gown to shame. A twinge of jealousy scratched at her. Who owned such a lovely dress? Did it belong to someone Ian loved?

A voice at the door startled her.

"It was my mother's," a woman said.

Turning to the sound, Skye pressed her lips together and made no attempt to hide her embarrassment. "I meant no disrespect."

The young woman was strikingly lovely, with dark red hair piled high and eyes the color of a cloudless sky. Her resemblance to Ian was clear, down to the smile that graced her lips.

"No offense was taken. I am Maisie, sister to the laird, and our mother has been gone these many years. But these gowns were barely worn, and we hadn't the heart to give them away."

"They are beautifully made." Skye carefully refolded the dress and placed it back in the chest.

"I have heard of your circumstances and if the clothes fit you, please wear them. It would please me and I am certain it would please Ian as well."

"I couldn't. And I did manage to salvage another dress, but I do thank you for the kind offer."

89

"Well one or two gowns and nae a warm cloak will not suffice. I will see to your comfort."

"That's very kind."

Maisie strode over to the bed and sat beside the dog, who had been watching their exchange with interest. "Did you offer him a morsel?" Maisie asked, without malice.

"A morsel?" Skye giggled. "No. I think we just like each other."

"It's just that Dionadair is my brother's companion and has never really taken to anyone else. I am happy he nae longer growls at me or my husband." Maisie laughed. "I suppose it is the nature of the beastie." Maisie cocked her head. "But he has certainly been drawn to you. Perhaps it is an omen."

Skye laughed. "That's what Neasa said." *Could this really be happening?*

Maisie leaned in conspiratorially. "My brother needs a wife and there are none here who suit him. But he looked at you as if you were a delicacy he longs to sample." Maisie shrugged. "I would not like to see him hurt." The tone was steel beneath the words.

Skye knew that if she were too anxious after so short a time, it might look suspicious. There is no way Maisie or anyone else here could know she had been obsessed with the man for weeks. Or at least, obsessed with his image.

"I..." Skye bit her lip. "Your brother is a trés attractive man."

Maisie smiled. "That is indeed a good beginning." Standing, Maisie held out her hand. "I hope we will be friends."

"I would like that."

Chapter Nine

Carefully placing her bag at the bottom of the chest, she covered it with the gowns, taking a moment to appreciate the beauty and workmanship of the garments. Ian and Maisie's mother clearly had excellent taste and Skye wondered why and how she had died. Maisie said it was years ago, so the woman must have died young. Of course, without modern medicine, even the simplest illness or injury could prove fatal.

The thought sent a shiver up her spine. What had she gotten herself into? But, she always had the cloak and could go back. Go back to what, was the question. No, her fate was here, the chance to be with the love of her life. And that was worth any risk.

Closing the box and wishing she could lock it, Skye decided this was a wonderful opportunity to explore her new surroundings, and continue reassuring herself this was all real.

When she reached the base of the steps, a very tall, well-built young man stepped up to her. His long auburn hair and green eyes suggested he might not be directly related to Ian, but even distant cousins qualified as immediate family here.

He bowed from the waist and grinned at her. "I am Conall, from the most handsome branch of the MacKenzies, and right hand to the laird."

"And obviously the most modest branch," Skye responded.

"That, too," he said, his grin widening. "May I offer my services, my lady." He winked and Skye could not help but laugh out loud.

"Thank you, sir, but I just thought I would take a…" She hesitated, searching for the word meaning walk. "A dauner."

"I could accompany you, if you like." He looked over her shoulder. "Dionadair?"

"We have grown quite attached," Skye said.

"Does Ian know, since he might be a bit put out. The dug never leaves his side. Until now."

Skye smiled and turned to look at the dog. "Aren't you supposed to be with your master?"

Dionadair lowered his ears, wagged his tail, and quickly scampered off. Skye grinned and Conall offered his arm, escorting her through the main hall and out into the courtyard.

Skye was again amazed at her surroundings. People were everywhere, immersed in their various tasks. People in fabulous costumes. Still so hard to accept. Sounds of fighting in the distance caught her attention and she stiffened, her mouth agape. Knowing from history that men in this time trained constantly was very different than hearing the clanging of swords on metal.

"Do they not practice in France?" Conall asked.

Embarrassed, Skye nodded. "Of course. I suppose after the attack on my men, I am just a bit on edge."

"Forgive me. I should be more sensitive." He patted her hand. "Let me show you where our wummin make cloth."

Stepping in front of them was a man built like a tree trunk. His hair was long, too, but black and his blue eyes were in stark contrast to his sun darkened skin. Handsome in a rugged way, Skye's first impression was that Harper would be disarmed at the sight of him. She had no doubt Harper's friend Jeff would look like a miniature in comparison. "I heard a lady had come to the castle." Angling his head at Conall, he glared. "Did ye think to keep her all to yerself? Or will you introduce me proper?"

"My lady Skye, may I present the great unwashed Daimh. His name means ox. Suitable as you can see. Now off you go, mon. I have a tour to conduct."

Grumbling under his breath, Daimh reluctantly walked away.

"He is harmless, unless of course there is a threat. I, on the other hand, am a lover, nae a fighter."

"Did you not just come from a battle to save our queen?" Skye teased.

"Aye, but that was, as ye said, a battle, and nae the same thing."

***

Strolling back from the smithy, Ian stopped when he saw the lady across the inner courtyard with Conall. A feeling he didn't recognize made his blood run hot. He should be the one escorting her, introducing her. He was laird here. It was his—duty.

Stomping his way over to the two, he intercepted them as they approached the weaving shed. Dionadair raced from his side to greet the lady, which only increased Ian's annoyance. Could he count on loyalty from no one?

"Laird," Conall greeted him.

"Conall." The irritation in his tone was obvious and Ian noticed Skye's cheeks flushed.

93

"I was just showing the lady about."

"I can see that. But have ye not some tasks to tend? Some training?"

Conall blinked at him, then smiled. "Mayhap you should do the honors then. As laird." He ducked his head in an abbreviated bow.

"Yes." Ian stepped forward and took hold of Skye's hand, placing it in the crook of his own elbow. "And you need not wink at the lass."

Skye nearly burst out laughing at that. Obviously Conall's tricks preceded him.

Walking away, Conall stopped and turned. "Laird, I was wondering if I might approach you later about a matter most private."

"That might be a welcome idea." He would be able to calmly explain to Conall that he had every intention of entertaining this lass without any help. And, if there was any confusion, Ian would break his head.

***

It was truly like moving in a dream. From the minute she laid eyes on the man, first in the portrait and then in the flesh, Skye had been captivated. Now, holding his arm and walking about the castle grounds, she forced herself to try and embrace the reality. This was all genuine, she was in 1562 Scotland, they had bought her story of how she had come to be here, and he actually seemed as attracted to her as she was to him.

He was proud of his clan and his castle, as well he should be. Their history was harsh and full of conflict, and yet the peace here inside the castle walls now pervaded. Each member of the clan had a task, and everyone supported the whole. And all would fight to defend it.

As people approached them, their curiosity obvious, Ian would introduce them, answer the questions asked and address whatever problems were brought. It was obvious how respected he was, and she was duly impressed.

As they explored the area, there was still the feeling of being in a dream. But the strength of his arm through his linen shirt and the heat that radiated from his body convinced her that this was not merely a figment of her imagination. When he spoke to her, and smiled, her knees became weak, and Skye knew she was lost. It had only been hours, but she was already madly in love with this man. Of course, she had certainly already fallen for him the minute she unrolled that portrait.

"You must be tired," Ian said.

"I am, but not so much that I cannot appreciate being in the shelter of this castle."

"Ye have been through an ordeal and here I've walked your legs off. Perhaps in a day or so we could ride about the countryside. It is pleasant this time of year." He cocked his head at her.

Luckily, she had taken riding lessons for years and felt comfortable on the back of a horse. In fact, it was one of her pleasures since she was young. Even when money was tight, she managed to always have enough for that activity.

"I would like that very much."

"Can ye ride astride? We have none of those fancy sidesaddles here."

Thank heaven. "I prefer it."

"'Tis time for the evening meal. Come and sit beside

95

me and tell me what appealed to you about life in the French court. Or what will now be the Scottish court."

Skye grinned at him. "Somehow I think you care naught for the French or any other court. You do not strike me as a man who prefers the pomp and ceremony."

Returning her grin, he nodded. "Ye already know me."

If he only knew the truth. Skye had spent hours of research learning about the culture and ways of medieval Scotland. And the lairds. But she was anxious to learn more about this man who had captured her soul.

Hesitating, he inhaled deeply. "And if you were never to be part of the court, but instead remained in a place such as this, would you be disappointed?"

Trying not to sound too anxious and getting a firm grip on her emotions while attempting to keep from drowning in those amazing eyes of his, she licked her lips and swallowed. "This life—the one you and your clan have created here—holds much to recommend it."

Reaching across and squeezing her hand, still resting in the crook of his arm, displayed his pleasure at her response. Leading her into the main hall, he directed her to the seat beside his own.

***

Beautiful, and with a gentleness that clearly belied great inner strength, this woman impressed him more each moment. She had survived an attack, found her way here on her own, and not a single complaint passed her lips. When she met the members of his clan, she was warm and gracious and kind.

Worry tightened his brow. When he had asked her about staying here, she had not appeared to be frightened off at the notion, but he feared moving too fast was never a good idea.

There was simply something about this woman that made him feel he had known her all his life. Every instinct he had whispered he should just carry her to the chapel and marry her tonight. But that was ridiculous. He barely knew her, and he might need permission from the queen, since Lady Skye was committed to serving her. He wouldn't offend his queen for any reason, but after the battle at Inverness, he was certain the queen would not deny him. Especially since Skye hadn't already been accepted into the queen's service.

His gaze moved from her pink lips to the cleavage that suggested the fullness of her creamy breasts and Ian had to shift uneasily in his seat. It would be unseemly to reveal his arousal. But the larger question was if this was a woman who could sit beside him, be his helpmate with the clan, and bear his children? The very idea of creating those children was almost more than he could stand, so he turned his attention to the food before him.

Watching her as she slipped a wee bite into her lush mouth made his discomfort worse and he was thrilled when Conall approached him.

"Laird, if I might have a word after the meal."

Conall was as loyal a member of this clan as any ever born, but Ian feared he was going to ask after Lady Skye. He dreaded a rift with his friend, but there was no way he was ever going to step aside. Best he dealt with the matter as soon as possible.

Giving himself a minute, he was able to stand without embarrassment and indicated he and Conall should move close to the fireplace where no one would overhear them.

"Laird, I cannot help but notice your attraction to the Lady Skye."

Ian narrowed his eyes defensively. "And…"

"Well I was wondering… hoping… that since she is not of interest to you now…" Conall hesitated and now Ian was completely confused. "Although I do not think she ever was."

"Speak clearly, man."

"Well, I would like to pursue Davina."

Ian nearly burst out laughing with relief. That would certainly solve two problems and Ian couldn't be happier. "With my blessing." He nearly shouted the words as he slapped Conall on the back, nearly knocking the other man over. "But ye ken you might have competition from wee Rory."

"The stableboy?"

"He pants after her like a dug in heat."

"So do all the young boys when they get a peek at what she reveals below her neckline."

"She also has a reputation of—ambition." Ian wanted to be diplomatic, but the truth was Davina was headstrong and selfish. And, he had seen the evidence of this growing worse over the years.

"I know she can be difficult, but I cannot seem to control my heart."

"Is it your heart, man? Or something lower?"

"I suppose I willnae know unless I pursue her, aye?"

"Good luck to you, Conall. Ye definitely have my permission. But do be cautious."

"I am not like the untried lads. I know she flaunts what she has, but I think she does nae follow through."

"Come, let's toast to it, then."

The men returned to the table and reached for their mugs of ale, holding them high.

"May our future endeavors be successful," Ian announced, as the others joined him and quaffed their drinks.

Out of the corner of his eyes, Ian saw it coming, but was helpless to prevent it. Watching Davina lurch forward with the full pitcher, he cringed as the liquid doused Skye, soaking her.

Jumping up in outrage, Skye quickly gained control as she flung the soaked strands of her hair off her face.

"Oh, forgive me, my lady. It was an accident." Her insincerity was obvious.

"No doubt," Skye responded, holding her sarcasm. "If you will excuse me, Laird, I must change my gown."

With all the ladylike attitude she could muster, Skye stepped away from the table and made her way up the steps. Ian appreciated the sway of her hips as she moved away, but he appreciated more that she did not take the offending pitcher and break it over Davina's head. She was truly a lady, and he realized he had already made the decision to make her his.

***

That little bitch. Could she be more obvious? Skye had found herself competing with a mean girl, who had the subtlety of a brick wall. *Well, Ms. Davina, I have come a very long way and I have no intention of letting your dirty tricks discourage me.*

Skye regretted not actually being a witch who could cast a nasty spell and make Davina disappear. Or turn her into a frog. That would be fun. Then again, did Skye think she could just waltz into the castle and claim the laird without any resistance? They had both had lives—very different lives—up until now.

99

Shimmying out of the wet garment, Skye laid it on the chair in front of the fire to dry. When she opened the chest to retrieve her bag, she immediately knew something was amiss. Someone had rifled through this box and opened her bag. Her heart stopped. With shaking fingers, she opened the case and was relieved to see the lining was intact and her cloak was still there. Pulling out the chemise she slept in, Skye noticed her lotion and deodorant, which had not been hidden, were missing. Grateful she had the foresight to buy some old glass containers and transfer the contents before packing them, rather than plastic which would accuse her, she was still annoyed that these items had been taken. And she knew without a doubt who had taken them.

Stepping out of her shoes, Skye looked down and had a moment of panic. Her toenails were polished. Red. How could she have forgotten something so important? How in the name of all that was holy could she explain that? Nail polish wouldn't come into common use for centuries.

Discretion was the better part of valor, and she decided she would have to hide her toes at all costs until the polish wore off.

Slipping into the nightgown, Skye closed the chest, and moved to the door. Before she could open it, a knocking startled her. Quickly sliding into her slippers and wrapping a blanket around herself, she hurried to the door and was very pleasantly surprised to see Ian on the other side.

"Laird?"

"I came to assure that you were—unharmed."

Skye laughed out loud. "It will take more than a little shower of ale to be the end of me. I do appreciate your concern."

"We both know it wasn't the liquid—it was the intent. I fear that Davina believes she should have some claim on me."

Skye raised an eyebrow. "And I take it she does not."

He shook his head. "No, she does not. In fact, I just gave my blessing for another to seek her attention."

Although Skye had thought as much, it was a great relief to hear Ian voice it.

Clearing his throat, he straightened his shoulders. "I was hoping we could ride on the morrow, but I have just been told the Munro's are raiding our borders again and stealing our sheep. We leave now to catch them and remind them not to take what is not rightfully theirs. I am unsure of the time of our return."

The thought of his engaging in fighting constricted her throat. "You will take care?"

"You confidence in my abilities is not reassuring, my lady," he said, his tone teasing. "Trust that MacKenzies do not suffer trespass and it is the offender who will need prayers."

Without thinking, Skye stepped up to him on tiptoes and placed a gentle kiss on his cheek. Reaching out, he stroked his knuckles along her jawline. "Worry not. I will return."

He turned and strode down the stairs, leaving her skin burning from his touch. She leaned against the door and sighed. If this was a dream, she hoped never to wake up.

A scratching at the door announced that Dionadair was not content to stay away. Smiling, Skye opened the door and the little black dog strutted in and popped up onto the bed. She laughed out loud as he stretched out and made himself comfortable.

Closing the door, Skye realized she was absolutely exhausted. The idea of sleep, however, terrified her. What if she woke up and she was no longer here? What if this day had merely been a product of her vivid imagination? Like "Alice in Wonderland" or Peter Pan".

No matter how much she resisted, sleep would overtake her eventually, so she might as well give in to it. With Ian gone from the castle, she had to admit she was nervous. The memory of someone, and she was certain who that was, riffling through her belongings made her hair stand on end. Not that she had ever needed a man to protect her. Or anyone for that matter. A little precaution never hurt, though, and knowing the pup would guard her and warn her of any intrusion was comforting.

Replacing the blanket on the bed, she slipped beneath the covers, put her hand on the dog's back, and was instantly asleep.

Chapter Ten

Damn the Munros. So much for their recent alliance in defending their queen. And it was as if they had prior knowledge of where the MacKenzies would be. If they went west, the Munros would be east. When they rode to catch up, the devils were faster and melted into the landscape. Two shepherds were down already, their sheep gone.

Ian ordered the two injured men be taken to the castle, but he refused to give up just yet. There were still hours left before dawn lit the land. Stealthily, Ian and his men combed the landscape, their eyes and ears alert for any disturbance.

Suddenly, there! A flash of moonlight on metal and they had them. Circling around, they surrounded the raiders and the clang of swords against axe blades rang out. Shouts and cries of the fallen and the thudding as bodies fell to the ground. The battle raged until the sound of retreating hoofbeats echoed in the night air.

Quiet, except for the moaning of the injured and the bleating of the sheep that remained bespoke their prize. They had defeated the reivers and re-captured their property. Three lambs lay dead, no doubt trampled in the fight. They would not go to waste.

Several of the men gathered the remaining sheep as

Ian and the others assessed the damage. Breathing a sigh of relief, he noted that none of his men were down and only Conall had sustained a wound to his leg. Blood dripped down into the ground at a slow rate.

"Can you ride?" Ian asked.

"You insult me, Laird."

"Well bind the thing so you don't drip on the ground as we ride." Turning his head, he saw several of the men had the dead lambs slung over their saddles. "Let's go home."

"What about him?" Daimh called out.

"Who?" Both Ian and Conall asked together.

Riding up to them with a man slung over his saddle, Ian recognized the Munro colors. Lifting his head, it was clear the man was only a lad.

"The Munro laird's bairn," Daimh said triumphantly.

"I am not a bairn. I am a man," the boy protested, lifting his head. Fury stained his cheeks a deep red. Dripping with blood, his right arm hung limply.

Reluctant to insult him further, Ian thought about this for a moment. "Well, I suppose we should bind his wound…"

"And hold him for ransom?" Daimh suggested with glee.

Stroking his chin, Ian ruminated on the possibilities here. "We could certainly use him to negotiate."

Clearly recognizing the value of silence, the lad remained quiet as the MacKenzies galloped their horses back to the castle. Ian's first thought, as he dismounted, was to the safety of his men. He did not have to remind them to tend Conall and see him to Neasa, who was not only in charge of the day-to-day running of the castle but was also gifted as a healer. Several of the other men would take the dead lambs to the kitchen to be prepared for a celebration feast.

Dawn was just breaking, the colors of blue and pink and gray breaking through. Hurrying into the hall, he ran up the stairs to the room where Skye slept. His thoughts of her had never been far and he had been worried about her safety, which was a weak excuse. No one would dare harm her when she was under his protection. No, the truth was he needed to reassure himself she was still here. What if she had changed her mind in his absence and chosen to seek the queen and enter her service? The feeling of loss clenching his gut was not to be denied.

Quietly slipping into the chamber, his heart leapt to see her wrapped in blankets, breathing evenly in sleep.

***

Sensing someone coming into the room, Skye sat up quickly. Dionadair was wagging his tail, then slinked off the bed. Light seeping in through the window caught an apparition coated in blood. Terrified, Skye gasped and scooted back against the headboard.

"Lass?"

The voice was familiar. Was it a ghost? Did Ian die during the battle? Tears burned down her cheeks.

"No," she said, sobbing. "No."

"Lass?" he repeated, holding out his hand to her. "'Tis Ian. I have returned and just thought to see to you."

"Ian?" Skye blinked, trying to clear the fog in her brain. Her breath came in quick pants as her vision focused and terror took hold of her chest, squeezing. "You're bleeding?"

"Nay, not me blood." He laughed. "Have ye so little faith?"

105

Without thinking, she threw herself into his arms, the dirt and gore rubbing off on her chemise. She couldn't have cared less about the fabric. She was still here, he was alive, and it wasn't a dream. Shaking with relief, she pulled back to examine his features, then stroked his cheek.

"Knowing this is the welcome, I shall go to battle more often." Pulling her back into his arms, he held on tight.

"No. No more battles." But she knew full well another would come in a little more than a month.

Releasing her, he shook his head. "I have ruined your garment." His smile of appreciation at the sheerness of the fabric that revealed much belied his words of regret.

Remembering where she was, she scooted to the far edge of the bed. "Let me dress, Laird, or my reputation will be worse off than this chemise."

"Ian," he insisted.

"Ian," she repeated.

"I shall say I came to collect my dug, who clearly decided to be your guardian in my absence."

Dionadair obediently waited by the door, watching his master.

"Do not deny you spent the night here, you little traitor," he said to the pup, his tone teasing. Dionadair had the good sense to drop his head and whimper.

Turning to go, Ian looked back over his shoulder. "I'll ask a tub be filled so you can wash." And he was gone.

Her heart pounded in her chest. He cared about her. He came to check on her. This was real. Sleeping through the night didn't send her back to the present. Which was no longer her present. That was now, today. Here in 1562 Scotland with the man of her dreams.

Hugging herself, she started when a knock at the door announced a woman with a bucket of steaming water. Quickly covering herself with a blanket from the bed, she watched as the woman dragged a tub out from the alcove. Skye tried to help, but the woman waved her away. Two women entered with more water, and the three filled the bath. Thanking them profusely, they merely nodded in response, smiled, and then departed. This was such a rare and unusual treat. Expecting resentment that they were asked to wait on her, it occurred to Skye that they might be happy to serve a woman who served their queen. Or was hoping to. She had said she was of noble birth and that alone was worthy of respect.

Appearing in the door as the others were leaving, Maisie carried what seemed to be a bundle of clothes. Skye had put aside the blanket and Maisie gasped, then laughed out loud.

"Errol has done that to me more than once. They appear covered in blood to gain your sympathy. Disgusting. He has ruined more than one of my chemises. No wonder Ian asked me to bring you some clothes." She giggled and Skye joined in.

"I thought he was bleeding to death and came to say good-bye before he succumbed."

"My brother is the devil, but then, so is my husband." Shaking her head, Maisie stepped into the room and laid the clothes on the bed. "I willnae keep you from your bath."

"Merci for the clothes."

"Lady Skye…" Maisie hesitated.

"Let me guess. You wonder if the tale I told is true? Since I arrived here seemingly out of nowhere."

Maisie grinned. "It is rude for me to ask, but yes, is it?"

Skye nodded soberly. "I can give you my word that I traveled a great distance once I was alone, and I was as surprised as you when I found myself here. And it was indeed fraught with danger. I had no real idea what awaited me once I left home, but I am blessed that your clan took me in and has been so welcoming. This journey was not what I expected, but I am most happy it has turned out this way. Better than I could have imagined."

"That is good to ken. And I thank ye." Maisie turned to the door. "Enjoy your soak."

***

The warm water was delicious, and Skye took her time washing. It was early yet, and she could hear sounds below as the castle awoke and went about the day. She had no responsibilities and therefore no reason to hurry. Unused to being idle, she had spent her days in class or taking care of the apartments and she was at odds with laziness. Knowing that ladies of the court spent their time taking care of the queen's needs, such as wardrobe and jewels and amusements, Skye wondered what appropriate duties she could perform here to pass the time when she wasn't salivating over the laird. It was important she fit in as quickly as possible and allay any possible suspicions. Also, if she had value to the clan, they would be less likely to wish her departure.

Suddenly, it came to her. She could cook. Part of her classwork was studying the diets of the people through history and the Scots enjoyed a rich variety of food. The peasants actually ate healthier than the wealthier folks, since dairy and uncooked fruit was thought an inferior diet for the rich people. But she knew seasonings and she could bake.

Perhaps if she offered to share some recipes from her home in France—so that would be a lie, but these people wouldn't know that—she might be able to work in the kitchens creating some "new" and exciting dishes. That might make her more valuable and delay the need to contact the queen. She only needed enough time to make herself useful enough that she might convince Ian to let her stay. *As his bride?*

Dressed and ready to join Ian in the hall, she caught sight of Davina coming out of Ian's chamber. She had a wicked grin on her face and the hairs on the back of Skye's neck tightened.

"Good morning," Davina greeted her, too friendly not to be suspicious. She raised her shoulders and pursed her lips. "I suppose I have been caught in a morning's delight with my laird. Not that it's a secret."

As she scurried away, Skye could almost hear the other woman giggling. She pressed herself against the wall, her emotions ranging from disappointment to anger, and finally determination. She had come so far and prayed Ian would have an explanation. Not that he needed to give her one. She was the guest and had no claim on him. Yet.

The thought of going back to her own time never even crossed her mind until now, but she had to know if this romance was to be. Without Ian, there would be no purpose to being here. And if she had to go back, the thought of which saddened her very soul, she could at least write a hell of an historical novel, right? No. That would only make her devastation worse.

Hearing his voice in the hall as Skye walked down

the steps, it was obvious he hadn't been in bed with Davina. Unless they had a quick tryst as she was bathing. Her heart said otherwise. He had reassured her the night before that Davina had no claim on him and he didn't strike her as a man who would jump into bed with a woman while courting another. And Skye did believe Ian was courting her.

It would have been easy enough for Davina to slip into Ian's chambers when he went downstairs and then watch at the door for Skye to come into the corridor. Skye had to admit she was impressed. Davina's performance was Oscar-worthy. But the other woman had no idea Skye had traveled centuries to claim this man and had no intention of simply giving up. Still, a little kernel of doubt gnawed at her. Best to find out now if Davina was actually a threat, or just a woman with claws out.

***

Watching Skye descend the steps, he regretted his responsibilities. Determined to spend time with this woman, he decided that everything could be put off for a few hours while they rode through the countryside. The views were beautiful this time of year, and Ian was anxious for Skye to share them with him. Delaying his duties was quite unlike him, but he would make certain he didnae neglect his work, even if he sacrificed sleep.

He had asked that his horse be saddled, along with a very easygoing gelding. Not knowing how skilled she was on horseback, he opted for safety rather than speed, although he knew his stallion would be restless and eager to run. Riding horses to go from one place to another did not mean one was particularly accomplished.

Waiting at the foot of the stairs, he was surprised by the odd expression on her beautiful face.

"My lady," he said, "I have taken the liberty of having some horses readied for a ride. I hope you'll join me."

"That would be lovely. But would you prefer other company?"

"No." He raised a brow in obvious confusion. "You are my choice. Why would you think otherwise?"

"It is honorable to tryst with one earlier and then go riding with another?"

"Tryst?" He laughed out loud. ""Hardly, my lady. Daimh is not one to warm my bed."

"Daimh? But I thought…"

"I do not ken where you got the notion I was cavorting this morn, but I have settled two legal disputes and discussed the winter planting with Daimh."

Relief crossed her face and he wondered who had maligned him.

The smile that lit her face warmed his heart. "Forgive me. I was led to believe otherwise." She angled her head. "And do you ever sleep?"

He smiled. "Not when I must be awake." He took one of her hands. "Skye, we must agree here and now to always be honest with each other. It is the only way to build trust. If you doubt me for any reason, come to me before listening to idle gossip as truth."

"You are right, Ian. I was foolish and it will not happen again."

"Do I have your promise?"

"Aye. I promise. And the same goes for me. If you have questions, you must ask me and no one else." She hated lying to him. She dared not be completely forthcoming about where she came from. Some secrets were best kept hidden.

111

"It is a bargain."

Ian prided himself as a man who took control, but not in an abusive way. He merely did what needed to be done. He led her down to the loch and helped her into the boat. Dionadair hopped inside and made himself comfortable next to her.

After rowing across the water, he tied the craft, and together they walked a short distance to the stables and up to the waiting animals. He cupped his hands to give her a leg up onto the horse. She settled herself in the saddle and reached down to pat the bay's neck.

Noticing her seat, Ian wondered if he had been too cautious in his choice of a mount for her. She seemed perfectly comfortable and relaxed.

"I hope Morel is not too tame for ye."

Laughing, she patted the horse's neck again. "I find that most horses are very sensitive to whoever is on their backs. I have no doubt we'll do fine."

Trotting along the water, with Dionadair at their heels, Ian took more notice of the diamonds on the surface of the loch and the riot of colors splashed across the countryside ahead of them. Pleased that his land was so beautiful, he hoped Skye would not be disappointed by the views.

Riding in silence for a while, there was a comfort he hadn't felt in a very long time. It was a new experience to be with a woman who bestowed peace and excitement all at the same time.

"Tell me how you became laird," she said.

"My birth. I am the only son and my da was laird before me. It is not always the way here, but my father was loved and respected and no one challenged him when he named me his successor."

"The responsibility must weigh heavily at times."

"Aye. But the rewards are great. When I see a dispute settled to the satisfaction of all, when something comes together because the clan cooperated, when the harvest is good and our table is full—it makes me a happy man."

"But you must also lead in times of war."

"All men lead in times of war, in their own ways, when they or their families or their way of life is threatened. It is called courage and it must be mustered for any man worthy of the name."

Finding the place he sought, he stopped his horse, dismounted, and helped Skye down. They were high up now, surrounded by meadows covered in the glorious autumn colors of red and yellow and orange. The fog had completely burned away, and the magnificent view went on for miles.

Reaching into his saddlebag, Ian withdrew a blanket to spread under a tree. The dog turned in three circles, then settled at the edge of the blanket and promptly fell asleep.

"Does he go everywhere with you?" Skye asked.

"Everywhere but battle. Well, that is until you appeared. Now it seems he has split loyalties."

Skye placed her hand on her chest. "I did not mean…"

"Do not fash. He has good instincts, and it pleases me he is so drawn to ye. He has never done so before and I value his opinion." Ian smiled and reached across to stroke her shoulder.

Pulling a flask from his sporran, he sat and tapped the place beside him. Skye sat close and he could smell the sweet scent of her hair, the fragrance of her skin, and his senses sharpened with need.

Handing her the flask, she grinned, swallowed a draught, and coughed, tears running down her cheeks as obviously it burned its way to her stomach.

Leslie Hachtel

"Sorry, my lady. Not the wine you're accustomed to, no doubt."

Clearing her throat, she stared at him, but there was no heat in the look. Swallowing, she smiled. "I suppose I wasn't prepared."

"Do your lips burn?" he asked, hoping she would say yes.

"They do."

"See if this helps." He leaned in and his mouth captured hers. It was meant to be a soft peck, but when his lips touched hers, it was as if a flame sparked and ignited. The power of it caught him off guard and it took a moment to regain control and pull away. He had only meant to taste her, but this was—he could not even think the word for what had just happened.

"Forgive me," he said, his voice a whisper.

Skye was breathless. Then, her mouth dropped open, but no words came out.

Concern flooded him. "Did I hurt you?"

Blowing out a breath, she grinned. "Nae. Nae. I suppose I just wasn't prepared," she repeated.

"Nor I."

Reluctantly, he stood and reached for her hand. They must go back before this went further. This was not a woman for a quick toss. Skye was a lady, a woman fit for a laird as a wife.

Taking his hand, he led her back to her horse, and they cantered back to the stables. Helping her dismount, he whispered in her ear. "Perhaps on the morrow you can tell me more about you."

Chapter Eleven

Each afternoon, after the midday meal, Ian had managed
to slip off for an hour or so to walk or ride with Skye,
accompanied by Dionadair, who was either with one or
both of them constantly. Today it was to be on horseback
across the backside of the village. Skye was nervous
thinking about the details of her life that she could actually
talk about. Praying her memory was strong, she feared she
might contradict herself at some point and make Ian
suspicious. She had promised him honesty, but in this case
it wouldn't be possible. If she told him the truth, he would
not believe it. He would think her mad or a witch.

She had no sooner mounted Morel than the bay
started snorting. He had been the perfect gentlemen horse
and this behavior was unlike him. She leaned forward to
pat him on the neck and he tore out across the bridge at
breakneck speed. Ian kicked his stallion forward, racing
to catch up.

The bay galloped through the village, nearly
knocking over one of the local women, then tossing his
head, sped up even more. Sawing on the bit did nothing to
slow his motion and Skye was terrified. Once in the open
meadow, the horse reared, and Skye unceremoniously fell
off his back and slammed into the ground.

From a great distance it seemed, she heard Ian's

voice calling to her, bringing her back to consciousness. "Please do not die. Do not leave me. Not when I have only just found you."

Blinking, her vision cleared, and Ian was hovering over her, a look of sheer panic creasing his brow. On her other side, Dionadair was whimpering and licking her cheek.

"You're alive," he said, his relief evident. He ran his hands along her legs and her arms and checked the back of her head. "Where does it hurt?"

Taking a moment to assess her condition, it was clear that everything hurt. But she could wiggle her toes and fingers. She had hit her head and it throbbed with a thousand drumbeats. However, there was no blood at the base of her skull and for that she was grateful, but there would be a lump soon where it struck the ground.

She had fallen hard, but her shoulders bore the brunt of impact. "I am all right," she answered.

"Can ye stand?"

"I think so."

Very carefully, he assisted her to sitting, then putting his hands under her arms, lifted her to her feet. The world spun and then settled and she guessed she probably had a mild concussion, but concluded she had been lucky and would be fine. And she had brought some aspirin.

Leaning her against a stout tree, he walked the few paces to retrieve her horse. Once she had been thrown, Morel had no more interest in running.

"Easy, boy." Ian soothed Morel as he lifted the saddle from the horse's back. Dropping it to the ground, he saw something sharp sticking out of the leather. Cursing, he pulled a horseshoe nail from the inside of the skirt and held it up.

Then, checking the horse's back, he saw a long, deep scratch along the side. Red blood stood out in vivid relief against the brown of Morel's coat.

From where she stood, Skye could clearly see the wound. "I do not blame him. I would be frantic to get that off me, too. And the tighter I held on, the deeper it must have cut him. Poor Morel."

Slowly she approached the horse and nuzzled his soft nose. "I am so sorry I hurt you. You are such a good boy. I hope you can forgive me."

"You have naught to apologize for. You did not do this. But I swear I shall discover who did and there will be hell to pay." His fury was barely controlled.

"It might have been an accident."

"No. Someone did this on purpose and I promise I shall find the scoundrel who would risk your life and purposely wound such a gentle animal."

Skye had her suspicions, but how would Davina have managed? It would certainly appear odd if she were suddenly to take an interest in saddling a horse. Skye had hoped she only had one enemy here, but it seemed there was another who wanted to harm her. Depressing as the thought was, it was no different than modern day life. There would always be those who did not have your best interests at heart. She would have to be more cautious from now on.

Watching as Ian tied a rope around Morel's neck so he could lead him home, Skye could not help but admire the sinewy muscles and the sheer power of the man. Her imagination had not embellished how beautiful he truly was, even when she had nothing but a centuries-old painting to go by.

Helping Skye up on his stallion, he mounted behind

her and held her close, then took hold of the reins. "I will send someone back to retrieve the saddle. Poor Morel should not have to bear more pain."

"I agree." Ian's kindness touched her heart.

"Are ye sure you are not truly hurt?"

Skye turned as much as she could and smiled. "I've no doubt I will feel the fall on the morrow, but for now I feel certain naught is broken. My head aches a bit, as if I've indulged in too much strong drink. But I am certain that will be better soon." *Thank heavens I brought some aspirin.*

She could feel his attraction to her as they made their way back to the castle; nestled between his legs was electric. How she wanted this man and had since she first set eyes on his portrait. He was everything and more for her. And he was responding in kind.

As soon as they reached the stables, Ian bellowed for a groom. A lad ran out and from his reaction, it was obvious that Ian in a rage was a rare occurrence. Dismounting, he helped her down and turned to the boy. "Morel has been cut on the left side by a nail under his saddle. Treat the wound and send someone to get his saddle. It can be found under the large oak to the west, near the stream. And then I want everyone who was in the area this day to assemble in the hall. Now!"

The boy's eyes grew wide and he nodded. Grabbing Morel's rope, he stroked the horse's neck, then led him off. Another lad ran up to take Ian's stallion and he kept his head bent low. Clearly the laird's anger was an unusual occurrence, and no one dared incite him more now.

Later, as Skye climbed the steps to her chamber, Ian's words came back to her. *Do not leave me. Not when*

I have only just found you. She was hopelessly in love with him, and it was glorious that he had similar feelings for her. But someone was willing to go to great lengths to prevent the match. And she had a strong notion who that someone might be.

***

Ian had just finished telling Errol about the accident that afternoon and Errol was equally appalled. When Ian had gathered the grooms earlier, he could read from all their faces that they were all stunned by what had happened. In his heart, he had known the lads all valued the horses too much to ever do them harm. Rory had been missing, but Ian was told he had gone to get Morel's saddle. Ian planned to talk to the boy when he returned.

"All the stableboys blush when the lady is near, so I can't imagine they would risk her life. Or that of Morel," Errol said.

"Someone did this. And I will not rest until I find out who is responsible."

"I will be your eyes and ears as well."

Ian sensed her presence at the top of the stairs before he actually saw her. His gaze drawn to her, he watched her float down. The sight of her made his breath catch. She was magnificent.

Errol's elbow in his ribs interrupted his admiration of the lass. "When do ye think ye might propose a wedding?"

"It's a bit soon, do you nae think? She's been here but days."

"Why the hesitation? So unlike you. You have always been a man of decision when you see something

119

you want," Errol said, his tone teasing, while Skye was still too far to overhear. "It's clear ye desire the lass, and she is bonny. Ye said she was born in Scotland, which makes her less than a true *Francach*."

"I need the permission of the Queen if I am to take one of her ladies for a bride."

"Do you, now? Lady Skye explained she was not yet part of the court. If you send a message explaining the circumstances and must wait for a reply—are ye willing to risk the lass deciding to seek out the queen to serve her? Or the queen demanding the lady's request be granted?"

Was he? Ian knew from the verra first moment he saw Skye that he would have no other. Naught else had occupied his thoughts. He desired her.

Even in the throes of battle, her face had appeared in his mind, nearly distracting him. She was the one he had been waiting for all of his life. All he needed to do was claim her and bed her, so he could get on with his responsibilities. That thought tightened his loins.

Errol was right. If she sought to serve the queen, she must be of the one true faith, so that would not be an impediment. Common sense, however, told him he should not rush this. He would take the time to court her properly. How long could that take, after all? A week? Two at the most.

***

Ian patted the bench beside him, and Skye took her place. Clearly deep in thought, he seemed not to notice her intense perusal. Suddenly, he turned to her and smiled. The look he gave her made her feel naked and alive and heated by love. Taking a deep breath, she straightened her back and tried not to continue to stare. It was difficult because he was so incredibly beautiful.

"How do you feel?" he asked.

"Sore, but well. No need to fash. I am not made of glass."

"Stronger than you have been badly injured from such a fall. I will nae rest until I find out who is responsible. I have questioned the lads, but I have no villain as yet. But fear not. I will find who did this."

She reached over and patted his hand in thanks. He was so kind, so caring and just being near him had her heart soaring.

Dropping her head, she pressed her lips together. "I wonder if I might have a petit word with you after supper."

Skye was hoping to get him alone so she could ask about helping in the kitchens. The woman, Davina, was even now glaring at her across the room. Did the other clanswomen object to her presence as Davina did?

"I wished to speak to you, as well."

Her nerves sizzled. Had she offended someone already? Did another slander her? The one who tried to hurt her? "Is aught wrong?"

"Nay." Reaching over and patting her hand, he turned his head and returned to his thoughts.

Skye was reassured, but still nervous. Maybe they suspected she was a spy or not who she had said she was. Had she slipped up? Worries assaulted her and her appetite disappeared.

Finally, the meal was over. Standing, Ian led the way up the steps to his private rooms and ushered Skye inside. Frantically coming up with any excuse for his possible objections, her hands shook. Deciding to remain quiet until he spoke, the silence stretched on interminably. Her gaze moved about the room as she waited. A massive oak desk dominated, covered with papers. Several comfortable chairs sat in front of it with a dark leather chair behind for the laird. A doorway off to the right obviously led to his bedchamber and Skye shivered with pleasure at the thought of crawling into it at the end of the day with this magnificent man.

He had stepped closer to the fire and stood leaning against the mantle, his head resting on his right forearm, staring at the flames. Finally, he nodded, as if deciding something weighty and turned to face her.

"I was just wondering how you are faring now after your ordeals? First your attack on your way to the queen and again today. I hope the incident today has not affected your time here. It is important that you feel safe and protected. And I fully intend to see to it."

"I am happy here, Ian. And I have no doubt that I will now be under your protection."

Nodding, he smiled again. "I am glad you feel that way. But, you said you needed a word with me."

Before she could respond, a knock on the door interrupted them.

Daimh lumbered into the room, nodded an acknowledgement to her and stepped up to Ian. "The Munro lad. Do you have a plan?"

"See that he's fed and made comfortable. I'm thinking he needs to wed one of our own to ease the tensions between our clans. It is enough to fight to protect our queen without fighting among ourselves."

Did they mean to betroth her to another? Bile rose in her throat at the thought. Is that why he questioned her well-being? Was he going to suggest she stay on and marry another? And who was this Munro lad?

"Aye. Have you someone in mind?" Daimh glanced over at her, and she feared she might actually vomit. To come all this way for this? It wasn't fair. She opened her mouth to object, but Ian spoke first.

"I was thinking about the wee Elspeth. She's bonny and about his age. That should be a match that pleases the Munro."

"Aye. So we should send him home with a wife."

"I fear if we were to wed them now before getting Munro's approval, it might cause more trouble. We need to set up a meeting."

Daimh nodded his approval and left the room.

The relief that flowed through Skye at this exchange made her feel lighter than air. He didn't mean to marry her off to someone else.

"The lad?" she asked.

Ian grinned. "It seems we brought home a Munro son along with the sheep. The laird's own son, actually. But it's time for a truce. We share a boundary and combining our forces strengthens us both."

"And saves wear and tear on the animals."

"Wear and tear? Not an expression I ken."

Skye just shrugged in response. "You were saying before your man came in..?"

"The dug likes ye and he likes no wummin." Taking a step toward her, her knees grew weak and her palms damp. "I find it interesting." He cocked his head, his brows pulling together. "Did you wish to ask something of me?"

"I was wondering. I would be happier if you could find me some tasks for my time here. I am unused to idleness. And it seems only fair."

His eyes widened. "But ye are a lady."

123

"My parents were of noble birth, true, but I was raised to do my share and would feel better if I could help. Not all who are born to a title have means."

"Did ye have something in mind to do?"

"I find I have some skill in cooking, and perhaps could share some recipes from France."

He nodded, then smiled in approval. "Aye. That would be appreciated. I will have Neasa take you to Kenna. She can show ye what you need."

"Thank you, Laird."

"Ian."

"Thank you, Ian."

He stretched out his hand to her and she moved closer to him. It was all she could do not to throw herself into his arms, but damn common sense prevailed.

Just as she was leaving the room, a table caught her eye. On it sat a beautifully carved chess set. Stopping to admire it, she smiled. "Lovely."

"Do ye play?"

The intonation told her he had no thought that a woman could possibly hold her own in the game.

Her smile broadened. "As a matter of fact, I do."

"You are jesting. Women do not engage in this."

Rolling her shoulders back, she stood taller. "Would you care to challenge me, then?"

"Aye. Black or white?"

"Why black, of course. It is the stronger color. Just ask Dionadair."

At the mention of his name, the pup yipped once and settled at her feet.

Aware that he was looking at her with new eyes, she was delighted. The question was—should she kick his butt or let him win?

124

Chapter Twelve

Maisie met Ian outside early the following morning. Stress pressed a crease between her eyes.

"Out with it. I can tell when something is preying on your mind," Ian said.

"Errol says you are drawn to the lass. He said he thinks ye might be thinking to marry her."

"Does he now?"

"Is it true?"

"And if it were?"

"Do you not think you should know more about her?"

"Now I am confused. You seemed verra anxious for me to find a bride and get on with the business of heirs. Has aught changed?"

"Nay. I suppose I was listening to Davina, who has her sights set on ye. Word is the new lady wishes to take over the kitchen and make demands."

Ian couldn't resist a broad smile. "The lass asked if she could help out and earn her keep while she stays here. I think it is a grand quality to not expect to be waited on."

"And you think Davina is spouting bitterness out of jealousy." It wasn't a question.

"Did ye know Conall wishes to pursue her?"

"Lady Skye?"

"Nay. Davina. She could do worse."

"Ah, but he isn't the laird. And we both know Davina is… determined."

"He's a verra talented painter. I just hope he kens what she's about." Ian thought for a moment. "Have ye talked with the lass? Lady Skye, I mean. How does she seem?"

Maisie took a deep breath. "I have. She seems—charming." Angling her head, she grinned. "Ye did mention I might conjure a woman out of thin air. Will she do?"

He laughed heartily. "So yer taking credit for her appearing here, are ye?"

Maisie grinned and shrugged. "So, what do you think?"

"And why should she not do? Although, truth be told, I ken ye had little to do with it."

"There is something about her that strikes me. It's as if she feels out of place, unsure."

"She was on her way to a verra different life. Plus the shock of the attack. And I ken her life before was not an easy one. Losing her family to plague must have been terrible."

"True. She does seem to have a good heart and she is bonny. Her teeth are so even and white."

"And she plays a challenging game of chess."

"Nay!"

"Aye she does. I had to work hard to beat her last eve." Ian laughed out loud again. "And me dug favors her." Then, sobering, he leaned into his sister. "I must confess, sister, I hae never felt an attraction like this. I was hoping to marry a woman that appealed to me, not just one who would be a good breeder. But this woman…

every time I'm near her she draws me in. And I find I hae her in my thoughts when she is not in my sight."

"I am all for aught that makes you happy. But I want to be certain she willna betray your trust. She did promise as much."

He raised an eyebrow. "And this worries you? Does she strike you as a spy?" He knew in his bones that was ridiculous.

Maisie thought about that. "Nay, though she does seem wide-eyed and innocent, which could be a means of deception. But what would be the point of spying on us?"

"I would agree. Sneaking about to discover secrets here would be a waste of time." He inhaled and rolled his shoulders to rid them of the tension. "She knows of Mary and her court, which makes sense. I have no reason to doubt her story. But I shall be cautious."

Maisie lifted on her tiptoes to kiss her brother's cheek. "Good." Maisie turned to walk away. "I do like her," she said over her shoulder.

***

It was obvious which of the women was Kenna. She strode about the kitchen like a field commander, overseeing, correcting, complimenting. The place was a flurry of activity, but no wonder. They were feeding so many hungry mouths three times or more a day. Women were kneading bread, stirring soups in huge pots in one corner of the massive fireplace, while others tended to meat turning on a spit in the other corner. Skye's mouth watered at the delicious and savory smells.

When Neasa had brought her here when she first arrived, Skye hadn't paid much attention to the details of what was going on around her. Her head was spinning, and everything was surreal. Watching the women work in the tidy space was like watching a well-choreographed dance. A wave of tension washed over Skye. Could she actually fit in here? Perhaps she should have stuck to long walks and rides with Ian. But no, she wanted this to be her forever home and she knew she could not stay idle. She would have to make it work.

Marching over to Neasa, Kenna looked questioningly at Skye. Neasa did not bother with introductions.

"The Lady Skye wishes to offer her services. Coming from France, she could suggest some variety that might be interesting."

"I can bake," Skye offered. "Cakes and pies and the like."

Kenna ruminated on this for a moment. She was not a handsome woman. Young, probably still in her late teens or early twenties, and big-boned, she had stringy brown hair forced back into a cap and a hooked nose. Her pale complexion was highlighted with two round cheeks, her blue eyes sharp and suggesting intelligence and kindness.

When Kenna did not respond, Skye tensed for her reaction and was relieved when the other woman smiled. "Aye. I can use the help. And no doubt something different now and again would please the laird." Her direct stare at Skye suggested a double meaning. This was like a small town, where everyone knew everyone else's business. Her welcome was clear.

Slinging an arm around Skye, Kenna pulled her further into the room and began pointing out the various women and their particular tasks. Taking her over to the massive fireplace, she angled a huge cauldron out of the fire and reached for a long-handled spoon. Holding it out for Skye to taste the concoction, Kenna quirked an eyebrow.

"Do you have any herbs? And a little salt?" Skye wished the words back as she spoke them. How could she criticize when she had only just arrived?

"Elspeth, you heard the lady," Kenna called out, and Skye exhaled with relief. The girl hurried to grab some containers off a nearby shelf.

Shaking some of the herbs into hand and smelling them, Skye nodded and added a handful. Then, she shook a small measure of salt, knowing how dear it was, into the pot. Stirring, she held out the spoon to Kenna. "Better?"

"Aye." Smiling, Kenna pointed to the shelf where dough was rising. "Hae you ever added those flavors to the bread?"

"Why, actually dill is delicious in bread, if you hae any."

"Elspeth, get to the garden and bring us some fresh." And off the girl scampered.

So that was Elspeth. The girl was no more than a child of thirteen or fourteen. She had the awkwardness of a child soon to be a woman. So young. Skye wondered if she already knew she was to be a Munro wife. But then, such was life in the sixteenth century. A woman's fate was decided by the men in her life, to their benefit. A female was meant to be a plaything, a pawn, a breeder. Their thoughts, opinions, desires, counted for nothing. It was definitely hard for Skye to swallow after living a life of independence.

***

The days grew colder as September progressed toward October. As promised, Maisie had seen to Skye's wardrobe, providing her with woolen gowns and fur-lined cloaks, which was important since a part of every day for the last weeks had been spent outdoors with Ian. They explored the land across expanses of green, along the loch, rowed into the village and walked among the cottages. Some days they would ride across the countryside and Skye found she was very comfortable on horseback, even relaxed and happy. Always accompanied by Dionadair. Verdant green mountains loomed in the distance, most days crowned by heavy clouds that always threatened rain and nearly always sent a cold mist, but it did not dampen her spirits.

Skye was daily reminded the grass here was so green and lush it almost hurt her eyes and the air was so clean. Bits of heather hung on, sprinkling the landscape with purple color. In the woods surrounding the village, an occasional bright flower lit the base of trees. Breathtaking was the word that came to mind.

Looking over into Ian's sapphire blue eyes, Skye's insides would tighten. She had never been taught how to love. Her parents were so involved in themselves and their own lives, it never occurred to them they had a responsibility to her. Knowing what love should be and what she had experienced were two different things.

Harper was someone she trusted and cared about, but what she was feeling now, for Ian, was very different. It started as a fantasy, a crush, an affair with the impossible, but it had grown to an all-consuming passion she could barely contain. Ian was teaching her what it was to love someone, selflessly, completely. And, from the way he looked at her, touched her with his hand on her arm, she could tell he was feeling something akin to it. It was if an electric spark passed between them.

"Is this where you slept your first night," he asked when they stopped at the cottage one afternoon on one of their walks.

"Aye."

"Not what you'd grown accustomed to, I gather."

Skye smiled. "One night with a roof o'er my head was definitely an improvement after my journey here."

"You're an odd lass."

Skye raised her eyebrows. "Is that good?"

"Verra. I hae not heard a single complaint from you since you arrived. Impressive."

Leaning closer to him, Skye grinned. "May I confide in you, Ian?"

He smiled in response. "Always."

"I consider myself very lucky to be here. When I think of what could have happened after I escaped from the attack…" She gave a little shiver.

"Do not fash yourself, lass. I vowed to protect you and I will. I will always keep you safe."

Placing an arm around her shoulders, he pulled her in close to his side. Resting her head on his shoulder, she marveled at her luck. She was here, with him, the man of her dreams, and he cared for her. It was almost too much joy to bear. She prayed she could stay like this forever.

Strolling through the village still held so much unreality. The cottages, shops, architecture, even the muddy roads seemed taken directly from a movie set. Skye marveled at simply being here every moment. Smiling, she gazed at Ian, who returned her grin.

At that moment, a sharp bump hit her behind the knees, followed by a thump and a loud screaming protest.

Spinning around, Skye was at a loss for only a moment before she looked down to see a wee lad sprawled in a puddle and crying his eyes out.

Instantly bending down, she wrapped the child in her arms and petted his head, using soothing words to quiet his misery.

"Are you hurt?" Skye asked, her tone gentle.

A woman appeared next to her, her expression one of horror. "Oh, Laird, my lady. Forgive me. Brodie meant nae harm to ye."

Standing, her arms still around the boy, Skye smiled. "There is no harm done. I feared for the boy, but he seems well."

"But he muddied yer gown," the woman replied, clearly horrified.

Grinning, Skye reassured her. "A little mud is good for the soul." *And in the future, people will pay real money to bathe in it.*

"You are very understanding. He's so full of spirit. Sometimes he is nae careful when he runs aboot."

Looking down and lifting the boy's chin so she could look directly into his eyes, Skye shook her head. "Was I in your way?" Humor colored her tone.

Clearly baffled, the lad looked to his mother, who laughed. "You are too good, my lady. I will try to control him so such a thing does nae happen again."

"Truth be told, I have nae had the pleasure of hugging a wee one in a long time, so it was a pleasure for me."

Ushering the boy to his mother with a gentle push, the other woman curtsied. "Thank ye, my lady. Come Brodie." As they scurried off, Brodie looked back over his shoulder and winked at her. Skye could barely control her giggles.

"I suppose Scottish men are born with it."

"With it?" Ian questioned.

"The ability to wink and charm a lady."

Ian's expression spoke volumes. His gaze had softened, and he reached out to Skye. "That was a kindness," he said.

"He is adorable. I would have been happy to snatch him up and take him with us. Though I believe his mother may have objected." Skye laughed out loud.

"Do you desire children?" he asked.

"Oh, yes. They are so innocent and see the world through new eyes. I hope someday to have many."

Frowning, he looked at her. "How many?"

"A hundred or so," she teased.

"Then you must find yourself a very rich husband." There was definitely laughter beneath his solemn words.

***

As they returned to the castle, they were greeted by Neasa, obviously in a flurry.

"Laird, I am at a loss with Elspeth. She's creating quite the stir. And we can nae get her to stop crying."

Cocking his head, realization dawned. "This is because of her betrothal to young Munro."

"Aye. She refuses to leave here. She is verra afraid."

Stepping forward, Skye put a gentle hand on Ian's chest. "Might I help? Perhaps I could speak to her and ease her distress. I do know a little about finding myself living in a new place."

Ian looked relieved and, shooting Neasa a look, saw her respond with a grateful nod. "Yes. Thank ye."

"I'll take you to her," Neasa offered.

133

The girl was huddled in a corner of the kitchen, her face red and swollen with tears. Backing away, Neasa left Skye alone with the girl.

Kneeling beside her, Skye placed a hand on the girl's back, and stroked her. "Can you tell me why you are crying?" Although, Skye could think of a thousand reasons for the girl's tears.

Sniffing, Elspeth looked up and wiped her hand across her face. "I must marry. It is the only way to calm the storm between our clans."

Knowledge that the two clans would war and then unite over and over would not help Elspeth. Let her believe that this forced marriage would at least end the hostilities. "Are you afraid?"

Elspeth's expression softened. "Aye."

"Tell me what is the worst of your fears?"

"All of it. This is the only home I've known all my life. My ma died giving birth to me and my da—well, he has no time for a bairn. Although I'm no longer a bairn, I suppose."

"And are you afraid your new home will be unwelcoming?"

"I ken not what to expect. I saw the lad for a few moments before he was sent back."

"And?" Skye prompted.

"He was not hard on the eyes." Elspeth gave a little smile that almost reached her eyes. "When the laird returned from his meeting with the Munro, and they told me of my fate, I—." Sobs finished her sentence and fat tears ran down her cheeks.

"The Munro's will become your new family." Skye soothed. "I have no doubt the young Munro will be pleased with you. But, if they do not treat you right, I also have no doubt the laird will welcome you back with open arms."

"You believe that?" Her eyes widened with hope.

"I do. Look how they have welcomed me, a stranger."

"It is not the same," Elspeth sputtered.

"It is. And ye know the Scots are well known for their hospitality. You are a lovely girl and you will make a fine wife. They would have no reason to be anything but kind to you."

Elspeth wiped away the drying tears. "You think so?"

"I do. The laird would never have promised you if he thought for one moment it would put you at risk. You trust him, do you nae?"

Elspeth nodded. "Thank ye, my lady."

Skye gave the girl a quick hug and stood, but Elspeth stayed her with a hand on her arm. "One thing more, my lady."

Skye smiled encouragement. "Yes?"

"The wedding night. What shall I do?"

Skye thought about this for a moment. Who was she to give advice on such matters? But she could use her imagination. And she had to say something comforting. The poor girl was terrified. "Do you know about the mating of a man and a woman?"

"I have seen the sheep and the horses mate. Is it the same?"

"Not exactly. People make love face to face. And they kiss. And touch. It is pleasant and to be enjoyed." Skye's thoughts went to Ian and imagining what their wedding night would be like. A quiver started in her belly and spread outward. Yes, it would be pleasant, *more* than pleasant. How could it not be? She was madly in love

135

with the man and had traveled hundreds of years just to be with him.

"Truly?" Elspeth's eyes were wide with her surprise.

"You should think that this is the man who will be father to your children and do not be fearful of asking him for kindness."

Elspeth wiped away the rest of her tears and threw her arms around Skye's neck. "Thank you, my lady. I do feel comforted."

Walking away, Skye could not help but feel sympathy for the child. So young, and used as a pawn to seal a futile treaty with another clan. She hoped that the Munro lad would be good to Elspeth. Then again, this was not the world she had left behind and she had to accept the way of life here.

***

Ian caught sight of Skye as she was returning to the main hall. She spent much of her day in the kitchens, but he had made certain to claim time for himself.

The lady had proven herself to him each hour he was with her. She was kind to all the villagers, the clan within the castle, the children. The flavor of the food had improved, and everyone seemed happy. And she had the most luscious bosom and hips. Just thinking about her made him ache with wanting. He definitely wanted her. She was the wife he had hoped for, and he would not be content until he claimed her as his own.

Two weeks had passed, and he was out of patience with the whole courting ritual. It was time to declare his intentions. Convinced she would make a good mate and one equal to the task of becoming the wife of the laird, he wondered if she would pose any objections. If she had no objections to the union, he could get the priest to have a marriage contract drawn up. Ian was anxious to have her legally his, so he could get on with the business of producing heirs. The thought brought a smile to his lips.

He recalled her saying she was lucky to be here. Was that due to the trials of making the journey here? Or would she be content to stay on?

Smiling at him, she approached his chair by the fire at the same time Conall came from the other side. He was still limping slightly, but otherwise seemed braw.

Conall reached his chair first. "Laird, there is trouble brewing. A messenger from Aberdeen has brought word of a conflict between the Gordons and the Forbes."

Ian nodded soberly. "How fares your wound?"

"It heals well. And I am ready."

"Aye, good to hear. Where is the messenger?"

"He rode night and day to carry the news here and fainted when he arrived. As soon as he revives and has had something to drink, I shall bring him to you for details." A noise attracted his attention. "Here he comes now."

A scruffy looking man covered in road dust and dragging his feet shuffled into the hall. Looking as if he might fall at any time, one of the men strode over to help him and lead him to the chair opposite Ian. The man sat heavily and inhaled.

"I fear I bring bad tidings. As I am certain you ken, Huntly is no supporter of Mary. Even now he marches to Aberdeen with upwards of seven hundred men intent on the capture of her majesty."

"I thought we settled all this weeks ago in Aberdeen," Ian said, irritation in his tone.

"I fear, Laird, it will not be over until Sir John Gordon hangs. But, as enemies of our queen, I ken you'd want to join the forces to stop this treason."

"Aye. We will march to Aberdeen and meet these miscreants. And I thank you for the message. Rest and refresh yourself now."

Standing and facing Conall, Ian shook his head in disgust. "Will they nae cease? We must defeat these traitors once and for all."

"Aye."

"We need to call a meeting of the lairds. I wish us even better prepared this time."

"Consider it done."

"Oh, and Conall—how goes it with Davina?"

"Do not ask. She has her sights set much higher than a lowly painter."

"Then she is so much a fool. Perhaps she will have a change of heart."

"It's possible," Conall replied. "But then, so might I."

Ian smiled. "Good man."

Chapter Thirteen

Seeing Conall approach Ian, followed by what appeared to be a messenger, Skye knew enough to leave them alone. It was time to prepare the evening meal, so Skye walked back to the kitchens. She busied herself with seasoning the stews and helping baste the roasting meat, wondering what news the messenger had brought. An hour passed quickly, and Skye looked up to see one of the young men approaching her.

"The laird wishes a word in his chambers, my lady."

"Of course." Skye followed the lad up the steps and into Ian's rooms. He was pacing in front of the fire when she entered, obviously upset.

"Ian?"

Swinging around to face her, he stepped closer and reached for her hands. Guiding her to a chair by the fire, he sat across from her. Immediately, he was up and pacing again and a frisson of fear traced up Skye's spine, but she kept silent. Finally, he stopped and turned back to her.

"I had hoped to do this differently," he said. "But it appears time will not permit it. So I will be blunt. You have said you are happy here and I am in need of a wife."

Hardly romantic, but still… "I see," she responded. Heart racing, she couldn't believe it. Was it possible that her dreams were coming true?

"Nay. That didnae come out the way I had planned." He dropped to one knee in front of her and reached for her hands. "I ken we have nae known each other long, and yet I feel as if I have known you all my life."

"I feel the same." Skye's heartrate was in the stratosphere now, but she was trying to maintain her calm.

"I am not good at words like this, but I am hoping you will consider staying on here as my wife."

His wife? His wife! Skye took a deep breath. "Yes. Yes."

The look of relief on his face was almost comical. "Good." He stood and pulled her up with him. "Shall we seal our bargain with a kiss?"

He stepped closer to her and lifted her to standing. They were so close she could feel his breath on her cheek. He smelled delicious, of horses and woodsmoke and heather. His lips hovered above hers for a moment and then his mouth captured hers. Demanding and gentle, stirring and exciting, Skye pressed her body into his and felt his arousal. She wanted him more than she had ever wanted anything or anyone, wanted to mold herself into him and never part. He was everything she had ever dreamed of. In fact, she had traveled more than four-hundred and fifty years to be with him and it was worth every bit of it.

Her fingers wrapped themselves into his thick red hair and he cupped the back of her head, holding her ever closer. And then, too soon, the kiss ended. Skye was breathless, her knees turned to jelly, heat coalescing between her legs. Knowing she could not be more forward or be thought of as a loose woman, she controlled her instincts to rip off her clothes and his and let him make love to her here and now. It was an instinct she'd never had before.

There was pleasure in knowing she was a virgin. It wasn't because she had been making some grand statement—Skye had just always wanted her first time to be with someone who actually appreciated her. There was no doubt this was the man she had been waiting for.

Angling her head, she could see the effect she had on him, and it was exhilarating. He desired her and she could feel his need to claim her. Impatience would have to be held in check, but she was hoping the wedding would be soon.

***

Ian was amazed. Never had a woman had this effect on him. He had kissed his share, lain with many, but never was it so profound. He stared at her as if she were a creature who had bewitched him, even though he knew better. It wasn't magic—or was it? But not because she was a witch. This was what was written in poetry, sung by bards.

Invisible cords pulled them together and bound them. The decision to make her his was so certain, his verra bones vibrated with the knowledge.

"I see no need to delay if you agree. There should be no detriment to our legal joining, should there?"

"No. None. As ye ken, I was making my way to our queen, but I did not have the opportunity to make that commitment, for which I am very grateful now." The words lightened his heart even more.

"Then the contract shall be drawn and our priest can marry us in a few days' time. I wish to seal this before I must go."

"Go?" But she knew the answer, although he could not know that.

"I must go again to defend our queen. Back to Aberdeen, or rather Corrichie. Word is there will be an attempt to capture her."

"Will the cursed rebels never learn that men like you will defend our queen and protect her?"

What glorious support from his soon to be bride. He would miss her, but knowing she would be here and as his wife when he returned soothed his thoughts.

"When must you leave?" He could hear her sadness and it swelled his ego. She would long for him when he was gone.

"I must go in a fortnight at most. That should give the clans time to meet and agree on a strategy. I trust you will be safe and protected here while I am gone."

"I will miss you."

"And I you, lass. I think we should seal this with yet another kiss." He pulled her close and wrapped his arms around her, pressing her lush breasts against his chest as he took her mouth. He could hardly wait until he could see her naked before him and kiss every inch of her body. His groin tightened at the thought, and he ached for her.

His tongue slipped between her lips and danced with hers, the heat building until he could bear no more without demanding more. It was clear this was a woman of passion. But a thought troubled him.

When he pulled back again, he looked deep into her eyes. "It willna matter, but I need to ask."

Skye pressed her index finger to his lips. "Nay, there has been no one before you. I have not given my heart or my body before now. Dinna fash."

Joyfully, he pulled her against him again and kissed her hair, the perfume of it driving him mad. Stepping back before he lost all control, he walked over to a table where

142

a decanter and glasses waited. Pouring them each a dram, he handed her one and held his aloft. "To us."

***

The evening meal had been served and devoured and, with a fight to defend Queen Mary in the offing, the men were in a fine mood. As the trenchers were cleared away, Ian stood with a goblet of wine in hand and the company quieted.

"I have an announcement." He dipped his head in Skye's direction. "The Lady Skye has generously agreed to become my wife."

The sound of goblets and fists banging on the tables was nearly deafening as the clan approved of their laird's announcement. It was possibly only Skye who saw the tray fall from Davina's hands and her rushing from the room. She took no pleasure in breaking another's heart, but as the others quickly surrounded her and Ian with good wishes, she could not help but be thrilled by their acceptance of her.

When the room settled, Ian went on with his news. "Since we leave for Corrichie in less than a fortnight, the wedding will take place in three days' time. That should give you all time to recover from the celebration before we go to fight."

Guffaws from the company filled the hall. Then Errol stood, his cup aloft. "To my brother-in-law and his soon-to-be bride, may your union be blessed and as fruitful as my own."

More cheers echoed off the walls and one toast led to another until all had passed out or left to find their beds.

Skye was over the moon. But a wedding in three days? She would not sleep tonight.

***

Neasa was as excited as any mother of the bride. She and Kenna rushed around in a flurry of activity, making certain there was a feast prepared and the hall was cleaned down to the fresh rushes. Freya, it turned out, had a talent for sewing, and offered to find a proper gown for Skye.

Three days passed in a moment and it was suddenly time to dress and sign the contract and prepare to go before the priest.

Glowing with pride, Freya carried in a gown that was so beautiful, Skye's eyes burned with tears of joy. It was made of a heavy dark yellow brocade with a square neckline and puffed sleeves. The skirt was split to reveal a satin underskirt of pale cream. Gold embroidery adorned the length of the sleeves and the edges of the overskirt and carried up the stomacher to the neckline. A gold belt completed the outfit.

"Freya, how did you do this in so short a time? It is gorgeous."

Freya blushed with the compliment.

"She did not sleep," offered Neasa.

"I cannot thank you enough."

"I wanted it to be perfect for the bride of the laird," Freya said quietly.

"And it is perfect."

Skye's curls were piled on top of her head and threaded through with gold ribbon. She felt every inch a queen, but worry niggled at her. This was too good to be true. All of it. Was she just being paranoid, waiting for the other shoe to drop? Inhaling deeply, she calmed her fears and prepared herself to join her love in the hall in front of the priest.

Entering the hall, her nerves singing, Skye walked across to her waiting groom and the priest. Her gaze lifted to meet his and suddenly all tension left her. This was real and truly happening. Every difficulty she had faced, every stumbling block, was worth it if it brought her to this moment, to this man.

Reaching out his hand to her, she stepped up next to him, repeating her vows and absorbing his, her mind and her heart in the clouds. He slipped a ring on her finger, and she lifted it to her lips, her gaze never leaving his. And then they were husband and wife and roar from the assembled threatened to lift the roof from the castle.

Skye had never imagined such happiness could exist and she decided she needed to revel in it, not question her good luck or fear it would all be taken from her, as so much in her past had been.

Sipping some wine, she was actually a little nervous about what was to happen when they were alone. It wasn't as if she didn't understand about making love. She had even advised Elspeth. It was more she had always called a halt to it before it went too far and tonight it was expected she would say yes. And she would do so with all the joy in her being. Anticipation sent a thrill up her spine.

In the past, Skye had to admit she feared having sex with someone would make her vulnerable. There was no such hesitation with Ian. She was safe with him, protected. She had no doubt giving herself to him would be everything she had dreamed of.

There was again that feeling of unreality. Was she imagining all this? This place, these people, this man? Would she wake up in her small apartment with no more to look forward to than another estate sale? She decided it didn't matter. This was her reality now and she intended to live it to the fullest. Her only regret was she couldn't share it with Harper. Her best friend needed to believe in magic. It made everything so wonderful. And she truly wished that for her.

Why, perhaps she could find a way to send the cloak back to Harper. It was about time her best friend experienced magic. Skye would bet Harper would fall in love with Daimh and live as happily ever after as Skye intended to. But, of course, the whole idea of somehow managing to get the cloak to her friend was ridiculous.

Chapter Fourteen

Escaping the celebration with his new wife, Ian wanted to make certain the witnesses to consummation stayed in the hall below. Before the union could be declared final, the bedding must happen, but he was laird and his word would not be questioned.

He had managed to secure a flagon of wine and, taking her hand, pulled Skye into his chamber.

"My clothes and things?"

"All here, as they should be. You are the wife of the laird now."

Catching her looking at the ring that now adorned her left hand, he smiled. "It was my mother's and her mother's before her."

Heavy gold, set with rubies and diamonds, it was a beautiful piece and it had given him pleasure to slip it on her finger as he spoke the vows.

"It is beyond lovely. I wear it with pride—and love."

Surprised to hear the words come from her lips, he raised an eyebrow. "Ye love me?"

Smiling in response, she sat on the edge of the bed. "Truth be told, Ian, I have loved you from the first moment I laid eyes upon you."

"Is that possible? Since I ken I felt the same about ye."

Stepping up to her and lifting her into his arms, he kissed her with all the passion that had been building for days, weeks. The little noise she made in her throat nearly sent him over the edge and he felt like an untried lad, experiencing lust for the very first time.

Determined to be patient and gentle, he had to contain his desperate need. Reaching behind her, he very slowly unlaced her stomacher, savoring the view of her skin peeking from beneath her now exposed sheer chemise.

As the top of her gown slipped away, he nearly gasped. Never had he seen such perfect breasts. Rounded and firm, with tight pink tips surrounded by the darker rose color, the pale cream of her flesh begged for his hands, his mouth. *Slowly*, he reminded himself. Kissing her lips, he moved on to the velvet skin of her neck and then the nub of her now hard nipples. He sucked on her and the sounds she made let him know she was immersed in sensation. But he had just begun.

Lifting her, he carefully placed her on the bed, then took a moment to look at her. So beautiful. Leaning over, he kissed her neck and returned his attention to her magnificent breasts.

The tip of his tongue made a damp trail down, across her stomach, to the dark red triangle that pointed to that place of ultimate pleasure. Separating her thighs, he sucked on the hard nub between her legs. She cried out, her hips rising to press herself tighter against his mouth. He drank her honey and her moaning spurred him on. And then, the waves of her release rocked her against his mouth. Since it was her first time, he wanted to make her as wet as possible, to ease his entrance inside her.

Eagerly, she reached for him, digging her nails into

his shoulders as he lifted and sank deep into the hot cocoon, now slick and welcoming. Feeling the resistance, he carefully pushed through it and, at the tension in her body, halted his movements until her body relaxed against him. And then she was pushing upward, pulling him into the welcoming abyss of her heat. All thought flew from his brain and there was nothing but need. Ravenous, driving need. He tightened his muscles, fighting for control. The tight restraint threatened to kill him, but he wanted her to experience more pleasure than pain. It was vital that she would desire him after tonight, and not just expect pain.

It was but a moment before her legs lifted around his waist and drew him even deeper inside her. He imagined he might just succumb to the exquisite sensations that rocked through his body as he moved in and out, until he knew she had reached another peak and he released his seed inside her. He pulsated until he was empty, but to his amazement, he was still hard and desired her once more. Knowing she would be sore, he suppressed his baser instincts and simply quieted his body beside hers, forcing himself to calm.

Soaked in sweat and exhausted, he was surprised to hear her laugh.

"My lady?" he asked, a little fearful he had disappointed her.

"If I had known it could be like this, I would not have waited these weeks."

Relieved, he kissed the tip of her nose. "I pleased you, then?"

She grinned. "When can we do it again?"

His laughter joined hers.

149

***

Most of the rest of the night was spent touching, kissing, exploring each other's bodies, and making love twice more. By the time the morning light slipped unwelcomed into the room, Skye was sore and absolutely satiated. Never could she have imagined this. Life, her life, before now simply didn't go this way. So far, all of this experience had been magical. Time traveling, meeting Ian, being able to love him and having him love her in return. Maybe some things were fated and the bad turns in her life were past.

Reaching over to him and feeling his chest move up and down in the rhythmic breathing of sleep, Skye had never been happier. Wanting this to go on forever, she knew that even if it ended today, she already had memories to last a lifetime. Deciding again to savor every moment, she smiled as his sapphire eyes blinked open and he leaned up to kiss her.

"I would stay with you all this day and more, but I do have responsibilities. So stop teasing me and let me be about them."

There was no harshness in his tone and Skye grinned. "But my lord, I only wish to…"

"After last night, I am clear what ye wish," he interrupted, grinning wickedly. "Oh, lass, I hae never been so drawn to another. Would that I never had to leave ye."

Slowly, begrudgingly, he sat up and swung his legs to the floor. Skye could not help but admire the muscles of his back that tapered to a narrow waist. The white slash of a scar across his shoulders gave her pause. Without thinking, she ran her fingers along it.

"Battle scar," he said, with a clear measure of pride.

"And the one who dealt it?"

"He will never deal another."

Seeing his healed wound did not reassure her. On the contrary, it only served to remind her he was mortal and when she first saw his face in the painting, he had been long dead for centuries. The thought shivered through her.

"Ye do not need fash."

Unable to express what she had been feeling, she wrapped her arms around his back and laid her head between his shoulder blades. "I do not like that you were hurt."

Even without seeing his face, she knew he was smiling. He turned to her and pulled her against him. "Ye will not be rid of me easily."

"From your lips to the ears of God."

***

Skipping her way to the kitchen after Ian left to train with his men and solve all the problems of the day, Skye's thoughts were on a new dish she had been planning. Well, new to her clan. Her clan. Yes, as the wife of the laird, these people were her responsibility as well. The thought filled her with purpose and a sense of peace. She had worried they would resent her presence and think of her as an outsider. But, with the exception of Davina, everyone in the clan appeared to accept and welcome her.

Kenna was barking out directions as ever, but stopped when Skye entered the room. "My lady," she said, tipping her head in respect. In fact, everyone froze and did likewise.

"Now, none of that," Skye said. "I am the same as I was two days ago. My name is Skye, and I am here to

151

work, just like the rest of you. So, let's get to it." She smiled at Kenna. "I would like to bake some pumpkin apple cakes, if that suits you."

Kenna grinned. "Yes my... Skye. That space over there is free." And the kitchen went back to the noisy bustle it had been before she walked in.

Putting her cakes on the shelf inside the fireplace to bake, Skye noticed Freya huddled in the corner. Glinting off her cheeks were the remnants of tears. Sidling over to her, Skye bent down and touched the other woman's shoulder, causing her to jump.

"Freya? What troubles ye so?"

Freya lifted watery eyes, her misery heartbreaking. "Naught to bother you, my lady."

"My name is Skye, and you are my friend. You created the most gorgeous wedding dress for me that anyone could hope for, and I am here for you. Now tell me. Please"

"I have my heart set on one who does not see me. He pants after another and there is no hope for me. He is making a fool of himself over her, and she is not worth it." Her voice had dropped to a whisper.

Freya immediately covered her mouth with her hand. "I should not speak ill of another clan member. It is wrong."

"Why don't we go for a walk and you can tell me everything."

Nodding, Freya stood and Skye, standing with her, took Freya's hand. They walked together outside into the murky sunshine, rain threatening and the overcast sky reflecting Freya's mood.

"It is impossible," Freya cried, new tears coursing down her cheeks. "But I love him so. Whatever can I do?"

"Hmm, let me guess. Could it be Conall who has stolen your heart?"

Freya gasped. "How could you ken that?"

"Your secret is safe with me. But he is verra handsome and talented, but he seems to be attracted to Davina."

"She is mean-spirited and does not love him. She hungers after the laird." Freya pressed her hands to her lips, the color rising to her cheeks. "I should not have said that."

"I am no fool. I have two eyes and I can see how she flirts with him. But he is my husband now and a lost cause to her. Which does not mean you should suffer if she turns to another."

"What can I do?" Desperation edged her tone.

"Well, I can tell you honestly that some things are worth fighting for, no matter how impossible they seem. You are a lovely girl, and we just have to make Conall see that you are the better choice."

"But how?" Freya asked, perking up. "I am not the kind of woman who could compete with someone like Davina."

"And that is why you will never succeed if you continue to believe that. You are just as pretty as she is, prettier, and your nature is one of kindness and caring. Those traits are so much more important. But first we must change your attitude."

"How?" Freya sounded both doubtful and hopeful at the same time.

"By changing how you see yourself." Skye looked her up and down. "Well, first the gown you wear is not the most flattering. With your talents, I imagine you could sew something more attractive."

"But I must work. Fancy clothes would just be ruined."

"Trust me, women can do their jobs and still look nice." Skye angled her head to the side. "And your hair. Instead of the braid wrapped around your head, it might look better done up in curls atop your head. It would still be out of the way, but it would definitely show off your lovely face."

"Why do these things?" Freya seemed genuinely curious. "Do you think it will gain his attention?"

"Feeling good about yourself is the first step to gaining anything, or anyone, you desire. The way you look is important. It will give you confidence. And men like that."

"Is that how you won the laird?"

Skye took a deep breath, then blew it out slowly. "From the first when I saw Ian, I fell head over heels in love with him and I determined to let him know how I felt. I know now he feels the same. I was so lucky to find him, but it never would have happened if I hadn't believed it was possible." *Of course, I believed so much that I travelled hundreds of years.* "When the emotion hits you like that—flutters, your heart pounding, cheeks flushing—is that how you feel about Conall?"

Freya dropped her chin and nodded.

"Then we must make sure he sees you at your best so he can appreciate you. And it is more than possible he will care for you in return."

"Word is they leave in less than a fortnight to fight for our queen. What if he never comes back and I cannot tell him of my feelings."

"You have to trust me on this, but I am certain they will all come home safe and sound."

Freya's eyes widened. "How could you know that?"

Obviously, Skye couldn't answer that, and she knew she should not have said anything, but Freya was so worried. "Just a feeling. I have a very strong faith and believe that God smiles on those who defend our queen."

Finally, a smile edged Freya's lips and she hurried off to create a new gown.

Skye was happy to have cheered the other woman up and Freya seemed satisfied with the explanation of the outcome of the upcoming battle. Skye was relieved, but she would have to be more careful in the future or she would raise suspicions.

Chapter Fifteen

Ian was as breathless as she was from their lovemaking. The heat of his body, his gentleness and passion were a constant source of delight. He was a haven she wished never to leave.

"Do I please ye as ye do me?" she asked.

Ian stroked her cheek. "Skye, ye are the joy of my life. Would that I had found ye sooner. Every moment with ye, especially naked, is perfect." Tracing her collarbone, he kissed the soft spot below her ear. "It's as if I have hungered for ye for a hundred years."

It was all she could do to hold her laughter. "I feel exactly the same way."

A thought occurred and he lifted his head. "I have been meaning to ask. What has happened to our Freya? The little mouse is so different."

"Should I be jealous?" Skye asked, teasing.

"Hardly. But she has gained the notice of some of the men. I told her she looked nice the other day and she said she had ye to thank."

"Can you keep a secret?"

"Always."

"She has her eye on Conall, and I think she would make him a fine wife."

Ian grunted. "So you think sometimes a man must be shown what is best for him?"

"You make it sound devious."

"And the wiles of a woman are nae?"

"No."

"You won me with yours. I was set on marrying one of me clan and settling down to a life without love or happiness and then ye appeared and showed me the error of me ways."

"That, my dear husband, was not deceit. It was simply that I knew I would make you happy, since I would move heaven and earth to make it so."

"Are ye saying you love me, then?"

"Yes, Ian. I love ye, with my verra heart and soul."

"And I ye, *mo ghradh*." He narrowed his eyes at her. "Do ye believe in fate? Since how else could ye have come here without the intervention of destiny?"

"I believe that when two people are meant to be together, it matters not what obstacles stand between them. They will do whatever is necessary to find each other."

"Then I shall thank fate every day for the rest of my life."

"Ye know, somehow I wonder how ye ken what is always the right thing to say."

***

The days passed in idyllic bliss, but the Battle of Corrichie loomed. Knowing Ian would not be killed did little to ease her mind. History reminded her the clans would cooperate and none would be lost, while the rebels would lose one-hundred twenty who would be killed and another hundred captured. Still, it was a battle and Skye longed to have Ian stay with her here. But then, if he did that, he would not be the man she loved. She had known

157

from the first that this was a man of honor who loved his queen and would always fight to defend his beliefs.

The thought of his being gone for at least two weeks was disheartening, but now she could wait for him here as his wife. How was it possible? Was all this real? Had she actually seen a portrait of a Scotsman more than four hundred and fifty years ago, fallen in love with his image and then traveled through time to find him? And then to discover he was as enamored of her as she was of him?

This was the stuff of romance novels. Of course, where did those writers get their ideas?

***

A clattering in the courtyard in the pre-dawn hours woke her. Peering out her window, the fog nearly obstructed her view. The men were preparing to leave but she knew Ian would not go without saying goodbye.

Grabbing a robe, she flew down the stairs, Dionadair at her heels. Nearly crashing into Ian at the foot of the steps, she flung herself into his arms laughing.

"Lass? Did ye think I wouldnae come to say goodbye?" He was holding her so tightly it was difficult to draw breath, but Skye didn't mind. Just pressing her body against his made the world right. Knowing he would be gone for weeks made the contact that much more precious.

"I will miss ye." Kissing his cheek, she buried her head against his shoulder and reveled in the closeness.

Stroking her hair, he whispered *"mo chridhe"*. Those words were true—she was his heart, as he was hers. Lifting her chin, he kissed her passionately, deeply, with all the longing they both felt.

Too soon, she pulled back and stared into his beautiful eyes. "Come back to me."

"Always."

And he was gone.

It was as if the earth had stopped its rotation and the wind held its breath, even though he would be back in a few weeks' time.

A shiver ran up her spine, as though a portent of some hardship coming, but she shook it off. He would return and all would be well.

The rhythmic sound of oars cutting through the loch and putting distance between the men and their home saddened her. Skye closed her eyes and said a prayer that the time would go quickly, since she missed him already.

***

The boats were barely out of sight when Maisie appeared behind Skye holding a piece of parchment. "I so hate it when they leave. I never get used to it."

Skye nodded, a tear slipping down her cheek. Quickly she wiped it away.

"And now I must ask ye if ye will be well if I, too, leave for a short time."

Skye tilted her head in question.

"It is my dearest cousin, Claray. She abides south of here in Kintail and is due to have her first bairn soon." Maisie held up the message. "She asks that I come and stay until she has given birth as she is full of fear, which I understand. I, too, was worried about me first."

Knowing how dangerous it was to give birth in the 1500s, Skye could not deny her sister-in-law the chance to offer comfort to another.

"Of course you should go. But you must know that when it is your time, we will all help you through it."

"I am wroth about leaving you here alone. There are no men and you being such a new bride of Ian and all…"

"Do not fash. I am a woman fully grown and know how to care for myself. With Neasa here, I have no doubt we will be fine. Although we will miss you."

"And I you. I already think of you as a blood sister and am verra happy you are wed to my brother."

"How long will you be gone?" Skye was a little nervous about being here with both Ian and Maisie away, but she could not voice that.

"I am thinking the babe will show itself within a fortnight, based on the missive from Claray. And then I shall return."

"Is it safe for you to travel? Will you have escort?"

"The lands I travel belong to MacKenzies and I shall take two of the stableboys. And I am not far enough along to endanger my bairn."

They hugged and then Maisie, too, was gone. Maybe that was the hardship Skye had worried about earlier. Well, she would be fine.

***

"My lady?"

Skye was on her way to the kitchen to break her fast when Freya walked up to her in the corridor. Skye looked at the other woman and blinked, not believing her eyes. The plain, unassuming girl had blossomed into a lovely young woman. Her red hair was gathered in soft curls atop her head and her hazel eyes were bright and shining. The gown she wore was of a soft, spring green that was form fitting and very flattering. It was as if the girl had been re-born into a confident, beautiful creature.

"Freya, ye look—amazing."

Freya's smile lit her face. "It was all thanks to ye, my lady."

"Please call me Skye."

"He noticed me." Color flooded her cheeks.

"Conall?"

Freya nodded so quickly her curls threatened to fall. "He told me I looked—different. As if he'd never seen me before. He was smiling. And he kissed me on the cheek before he left and promised to return quickly."

Skye was thrilled for her. "That is wonderful. Come, let's go into the herb garden and you can tell me everything."

As they linked arms and headed into the cold, fresh air, Davina cut them off. Dionadair had trotted up behind Skye and let out a warning growl.

"So there you are," she shouted into Freya's face. Do ye think because the men are gone ye no longer have chores to do?"

Freya gasped. But this girl had shed the skin of the mouse she had been. "Davina, ye are not the one in charge here. I take no orders from ye."

Before Skye could even react, Davina slapped Freya across the face. "Ye will do as ye are told." Venom oozed from her tone.

Skye immediately turned to Freya. "Are you all right?"

The girl pressed her hand against the wounded cheek and nodded. Then, Skye spun to face Davina. "Ye have seemed to have forgotten that I am the wife of the laird. And you will never strike another again or I shall see you severely punished. Am I clear?"

161

Davina did not even have the good grace to look remorseful. "Freya is a lazy baggage, and someone needs to see the work done. The laird will not be pleased to know you care naught about the keep."

Skye laughed out loud. "Are ye jesting? Ye had best find something to occupy yourself that takes ye out of my sight."

"Ye have no power here without Ian to back ye. And I will prove it to ye." With that, Davina swept away from them.

Freya's eyes were wide and her jaw had dropped. "Oh, my lady. Ye should not have provoked her. She is a powerful enemy."

Confusion made Skye hesitate, but only for a moment. "Is everyone afraid of her?"

"The wummin are. The men are too taken with her—well, ye know—most of the time to notice aught else."

"Does Neasa know that Davina terrorizes all of ye?"

Freya's brows came together. "I do not ken that word."

"That all of ye fear her."

Freya chuckled. "Nae. Not really. Neasa is much too busy to notice, and Davina is verra careful to stay out of her way. Neasa has sway with the laird, so if she knew, she would have the laird do something."

"So I imagine she thinks most of you stay out of Davina's way because of dislike."

Freya nodded. "And we are careful not to get in the way of whatever she desires."

"And she does not desire Conall, does she?"

Freya smiled at this. "I am lucky. She still has her sights on the laird, married or not. I think she hopes to scare you off."

At this, Skye chuckled. "Oh, then she has met her match. I love my husband with all my heart and nothing anyone could do will ever change that."

"It makes me verra happy to hear that. I ken the laird is happy with ye and you have already proven yourself worthy."

Freya threw her arms around Skye and hugged her. "Just ye being here has made me stronger." Then, blushing, no doubt for her forward behavior, she scampered away.

Returning to the hall, Skye sank onto a bench in the hall. Dionadair jumped up next to her. "So, not only is Davina a mean girl, she's a dangerous one, too," she said to the dog. He whimpered in return, as if he understood her words and sympathized.

"You will protect me, will you not little one?" she asked the pup.

His reply was a wagging tail.

"You know, I had a dog once," she said to Dionadair, who watched her with his large brown eyes. "In one of his few kind gestures, my father brought home a puppy for me. I loved her. But one day, he decided the dog cost too much to feed and took her off to the pound." Skye's throat tightened at the memory. "I never saw her again, and I miss her every day. But you are here, and I feel much better."

She wrapped her arms around the dog and kissed his head. Dionadair responded by licking her face. "I love you, too."

***

Even with the pup for company, the time from darkness to morning light seemed an eternity every night. The days were not so bad since Skye found much to occupy her time. She visited the villagers in Dornie and helped the women with their chores, cuddled babies, bandaged wounds, and cooked meals. At the castle, she still spent time in the kitchens, although with most of the men gone, the burden of cooking three meals a day was much lessened.

Skye was delighted to have time to try out new recipes and incorporate new food combinations. Without much sugar, she substituted honey and wheat was replaced with oats and barley. Since she couldn't set the oven temperature, she had to improvise by watching the baking of the bread and calculating the comparison for her cakes and pies.

At the end of each day, exhausted, she and Dionadair would find their way to her chamber and fall into dreamless sleep.

Oddly, this medieval way of life suited her. It would have been nice to have a microwave, hot running water, a flushing toilet. But the lack of these things meant nothing when she thought of Ian. She gladly gave up these modern-day luxuries to be with him. In fact, each day she grew more and more comfortable in this new lifestyle. It was odd how people could so easily adjust to a totally different way of life for the right reasons. But then, she had never been a stranger to hard work, so that was not a problem for her.

A full week had passed, and she hadn't seen Davina. Worried that this was a calm before a nasty surprise to come, Skye forced herself to focus on all the tasks that needed doing. When Ian returned, she wanted the keep clean and in order so she could not worry about chores, but rather concentrate on him. And she wanted him to be proud of her, that she had proven herself capable of managing the keep without him. Neasa was a huge help, explaining how the clan relationships worked. There was much to do to maintain the keep and it kept Skye gratefully busy.

Her thoughts of Ian were bittersweet. She missed him as if one of her limbs had been taken from her, but even in the short time they had spent together, they had made beautiful love. It was those memories that made her smile during the days. The thought of his return was a sharp sweetness she longed to taste.

Chapter Sixteen

After the battle of Inverness, George Gordon, 4th Earl of Huntly, was labeled an outlaw by the queen. In retaliation, he marched toward Aberdeen with seven hundred men to capture Mary. Word went out that their queen was again at risk and the loyal clans rallied to protect her.

Labelled the "Belligerents", the defenders outnum- bered the enemy and soundly defeated them, losing no men of their own. The battle was over almost before it began. A clash of swords and axes and storming an under protected castle was less than a challenge. One hundred and twenty of the enemy were killed, and another hundred captured. Huntly, supreme in confidence, was shattered by the loss and died of apoplexy before he could be taken captive.

Again victorious in defending their queen, the clans disbursed and headed for home. The Munros were heading in the same direction as the MacKenzies, and their laird caught up to Ian.

Ian slowed his mount to allow the other man to come alongside.

"Aye, Mackenzie, it was a good day for the clans."

"Indeed. So how goes your son now that he is marrit?"

"It was a fine choice as a bride, and I thank ye. I also thank ye, if I have not said as much, that ye did him no harm after ye had an opportunity to entertain him. Instead ye sent him home with a truce and a wife."

"It was the honorable thing to do," Ian responded.

"I hear ye have taken a wife for yerself. But that she is an outlander."

"Aye, I am indeed marrit, but she is Scottish born."

"So she did not just happen upon your holdings in a trip from France, as I heard tell?"

"Aye, that part is true. She was on her way to appeal to the queen, to be part of her court. Luckily, she made her way to Dornie after her party was waylaid. Brave lass. But what is still worrisome is that she was set upon by miscreants." Ian raised a brow. "Have ye any ken of how that might hae happened?"

Munro's face reddened. "Do ye dare accuse me of attacking a helpless woman?"

"Do not fash. It was a question, not an accusation."

Munro narrowed his eyes. "The truce between us is as thin as the line between our properties."

"You do not threaten me," Ian retorted. "I only seek to find the men who attacked my wife."

The Munro calmed and nodded. "I would feel the same. Well, if I hear any news, I will make certain to inform ye."

With that, the Munro turned his horse and galloped back to join his men. But he was right. The peace between the clans was ever a fragile thing.

The MacKenzies rode hard, anxious to return to home and hearth. When they stopped to partake of food and rest, Ian's thoughts were only on one thing: being with Skye and making love to her. It was a miracle she had found her way to Dornie. And alone. But then, she had already proven herself to be a woman of strength and

167

wisdom. He hadn't asked her the details of her travail, but he intended to when he was home. He desired to know all that had transpired, hoping the tale might give him a clue as to the attackers.

It was a blessing she had escaped unscathed. With her escort routed or dead, it was nothing short of a miracle she was able to maintain her innocence. And he could definitely attest to that. And thinking of their wedding night, his thoughts again returned to making love to his wife.

Chapter Seventeen

Skye woke one morning in the second week since Ian's departure and, looking over at her constant companion, she could not help but smile. Dionadair was a great comfort and it pleased Skye that he returned her affection. The pup was clearly reluctant to get up, but Skye was anxious to start her day, so she rubbed his belly and encouraged him to get off the bed. Dressing quickly, she made her way to the kitchens, the dog at her heels. She wanted to try a cookie recipe that would take some modifications, but just might turn out delicious. But she had to remember, here they were called biscuits.

Kenna and another named Isla who normally manned the kitchens were standing away from a table, eying something that was seemingly striking fear into their expressions. Two others, Sorcha and Alba, gazed at Skye as if she were a demon come from hell. Usually there were more women here in the morning, but perhaps they needed to attend to other chores. It was then she noticed Davina in front of the others.

"Good morning." Skye greeted them. No one responded or took their gazes from the table.

"What is it?" They were all clearly terrified, their bodies rigid with dread.

Kenna pointed at something with a shaking hand

and, unable to identify it from a distance, Skye stepped closer. Turning her hands palms up, she was confused. "All I see is a few potatoes."

"Potatoes? Potatoes! Poison, you mean!" Davina shrieked, stepping forward and shaking a finger at Skye. It was more than a gesture. It was a condemnation.

Skye bit her lip, then remembered that potatoes were not considered edible in 1562. In fact, they were thought to cause leprosy, be associated with the devil, and poisonous. So who would have brought these into the kitchen? And where did they come from?

"It was you!" Davina screamed at Skye. "I saw you consorting with the *Francach* soldier and he handed you a bag. A bag filled with death for us."

"Where did this happen, Davina? I have not left the castle." Skye forced herself to keep her tone even.

"I saw ye. Ye are a liar. Ye showed up here to work your charms on the laird so ye could destroy us!"

Before Skye could answer these outrageous charges, Davina turned to face the other women. "I knew it. I knew when she just appeared here. She was sent to spy upon us and kill us all. It's a wonder she did not murder our laird as he slept."

The accusations were so ridiculous, Skye was unsure how to react. Knowing that to get upset would be to fall into Davina's trap, Skye opted for a calm explanation as she shook her head. "I met with no Frenchman, and no one gave me the potatoes. I have no idea how they came to be here, but they are not dangerous. They can be baked or boiled and, with some butter and herbs, they make for a fine meal."

"See. She defends her poison, to convince us. She must think us verra stupid to believe her lies." She spun on Skye. "Then we shall make you eat them," Davina declared. "And when you die, we will know you for the spy you are."

Dionadair was sitting at Skye's feet and, sensing the mood of the room, let out a series of low growls. Skye leaned down to pet his head, but he was agitated and would not settle.

"Davina, I have no wish to harm anyone. You are my clan now. Why would I hurt anyone here?"

"Ha! So while the laird is away with the men, ye can rid yourself of all of us and allow whoever you favor to enter the castle and ambush the men as they return."

Skye's shoulders dropped in defeat. Logic would clearly not be successful here. "I will eat the potatoes and prove they are safe."

"That will only prove you are a witch. Only one practicing the dark arts could survive poison," Davina declared.

Nodding as a group, the other two women still looked nervous. "What if she does die? What will we tell the laird when he returns? He clearly cares for her." This from Kenna.

Neasa appeared at the door and stepped forward. "What goes on here? Davina?"

"We have caught the witch, the traitor, the spy who has tried to kill us all," Davina spat.

"What are you talking aboot?" Neasa demanded.

Davina pointed to the potatoes on the table. "We must stop her before she actually does some harm."

"That's ridiculous." Neasa calmly turned to Skye, indicating the potatoes. "Did you bring these here?"

"Of course not. I am aware they are thought of as dangerous here in Scotland."

"She lies. We must hold her for the laird's decision. I suggest the dungeon." No one protested Davina's statement.

"You will not harm the wife of the laird. I will not have it," Neasa asserted. "I saw no Frenchman and the lady Skye has said she brought naught into the kitchen this morning. Those things"—she angled her head to the potatoes—"did not come here by her hand. Now ye must stop this immediately."

Her words comforted Skye, but it was too late. Davina had stirred hysteria and it had gripped the other women, already escalating out of control. Their fervor heated the kitchen and they turned as one to Davina, looking for guidance. Dionadair barked, then bared his teeth at Davina.

"Yes! The dungeons! And get that dog outside before he follows her bidding and bites one of us."

Three of the women surged forward. Only Kenna hung back, her mouth agape. Sorcha had a length of rope in her hand, and Skye wondered where it had come from. Looping it over the pup's neck, she pulled him to the door and shoved him outside, then immediately came back to the group.

"You have no call to harm the dog," Skye protested, but her words were ignored.

"And take Neasa," barked Davina. "If she supports Skye, she is not to be trusted." She did not bother hiding the smile of satisfaction that curved her lips.

With a woman on either side of them, Skye and Neasa were pushed and pulled forward into the main hall and then shoved through an alcove, down a corridor and through a small wooden door bound in iron. It took two of the women to force the door open and it screamed its reluctance against the stone floor. Clearly no one had used this entryway for years.

It opened onto a black stairway that dipped into hell. Davina walked at the back of the group, now carrying a short sword that glittered menacingly in the meager light of the hall. A shiver of terror climbed up Skye's spine, and she broke into a sweat despite the dank chilling air coming from below. The reek of it permeated her nostrils and she could taste the decay. Bile rose in her throat and she swallowed hard. She refused to show her terror by vomiting.

Alba and Isla stepped forward and grabbed torches and, lighting them, led the way down the slippery steps, coughing as they went. The walls closed in, dark and foreboding, as they moved, and Skye saw both of the women ahead of her shudder with dread. The dungeons were not a place for a friendly visit, or a visit under any circumstances except the most terrible. Cold panic threatened to stop Skye's breathing, but she forced herself to inhale, exhale, and try to remain calm. But the shaking of her limbs made her all too aware that she and Neasa were going to be abandoned to suffer a miserable demise. Trying desperately to control the quivering of her legs, she placed one foot in front of the other, anxious for an escape. But she and Neasa were outnumbered and Davina and Sorcha both held weapons.

Davina was now in front of the group, opening a creaking metal door. The squeaking of scattering rats sent more tremors into Skye's limbs, and she longed for words that would stay this sentence. But none came. Reaching for Neasa's hand, the women gripped onto each other as they were shoved forward into the darkness.

A slick whoosh of air and Skye felt something

173

Leslie Hachtel

scratch her arm before she fell to her knees, the slamming of the iron door and the turning of the lock reverberating like the end of the world. Tumbling beside her, Neasa groaned.

The two were aware the others were disappearing up the corridor and it took every bit of control for Skye not to beg for mercy, knowing no quarter would be given. Davina had convinced the others they were saving the clan and they followed without question.

No fresh air, only a small slot far up on the ceiling for light, no possible way out. Their only hope was that they would not die before Ian returned. All that remained was to not lose faith.

"Oh, no," Skye moaned as she twisted back against the damp stone wall.

"What is it?" Neasa asked.

"She cut me."

Neasa moved closer. "Where?"

"My arm. It bleeds. I don't believe the wound is too deep, but I have no doubt it will fester."

"Aye. And here I have naught to treat it. But we need to bind it." The fabric tearing seemed to echo in the dank cell. "I have a strip from me skirt. Hold out yer arm."

Skye did as she was told and winced as Neasa probed for the wound and the cloth tightened around it."

"How bad is the pain," Neasa asked.

"The adrenaline is holding it at bay, but I fear it will start to throb."

"The what?"

Damn. No one in 1562 Scotland knows about adrenaline. "It is a French term for when you are fearful and do not feel pain right away." Skye hoped that covered her slip of the tongue.

"Oh, aye. I know of that." Neasa nodded her head. 'But I believe you are right about the festering."

"Is there a way out of here?" Already knowing the answer, Skye asked the question anyway.

Neasa huffed a sigh. "These dungeons have nae been used for years. In truth, I forgot they were here. But I do know they were built to hold enemies and even torture them." Neasa sniffed, holding back tears. "No. I can nae imagine there is escape."

Skye slowly stood, her knees scraped raw from her fall forward. *Great, more infection.* Feeling her way along the walls, the moss and damp soon coated her palms. Wiping her hands on her skirt, she continued around until she reached the bars. Set deep in blocks of stone, even after so many years, they showed no evidence of enough decay to be weakened. Neasa was right. They were trapped.

Skye gathered her courage and took a deep breath. "Ian should be back in a sennight or less. He will speak for us, save us. He loves us and I know he trusts you. He will not believe I would have any motive for treachery." Skye rubbed Neasa shoulders and was impressed by the rigidity of the other woman's spine.

"We will not give in," Neasa said. "Davina has plotted this and she willnae get away with it."

"This is all my fault. You are here because of me." Skye choked back a sob.

"Nay. Davina had always had a grudge against me. I find her loathsome and she kens it."

"How did she find potatoes?"

"Probably sent the lad, Rory, to find them. He would do anything she asked, lovesick as he is."

"Well, they are not dangerous. In fact, they will be a staple in the kitchen before long."

Neasa said nothing for a moment. "How could you know that?"

Damn. Skye had been so careful until now. She had watched virtually every word, but this simple error would only serve to make Neasa suspicious. If she lost her only ally, she would be bereft. She needed a plausible explanation and quick. She dare not tell the truth of how she knew, or Neasa would surely think her mad. Or a witch.

Feeling for the wall again, and disgusted by the touch of its slimy dampness, Skye knew they could not continue to stand up. They would have to sit, as loathsome as the possibility was. So, she sank to the cold stone floor.

"Please come sit with me," Skye ventured. "I can share much of what I learned all those years in France."

Clearly reluctant to sink down onto the disgusting floor, Neasa slowly eased herself into a sitting position, knees bent.

"In France, we ate potatoes all the time. They are not harmful. The idea that they were poison arose because someone of English rank ate the berries from the plant and got sick. The edible part grows beneath the ground. It was ordered that the plant should be burned and a servant, brave soul that he was, tasted the underground part after it was cooked. The servant found it delicious, not harmful at all, but the rumors persisted."

Neasa cleared her throat "Did you bring them here? Innocently?"

"Nay. I would not do that. I know they are thought dangerous here. It was another who wished to place the blame on me."

Neasa dropped her head. "I'm sorry. I shouldnae have even doubted you for a moment."

"Neasa, will they let us die here?"

Neasa shook her head. "I ken not. Davina can be a vicious adversary and you have taken what, or rather, who she desired most in the world. She is used to getting her own way. I have nae doubt she will have already come up with a plausible explanation for sending us to the dungeons when the laird returns."

"Can you ever forgive me? This is all my doing. Yer being here." The guilt to have this kind woman share her punishment made Skye sick.

Neasa reached for Skye's hand and squeezed. "Nae. If Davina had become the wife of the laird, she would have found another way to rid herself of me. She desires to be in control and anything less is not acceptable." Neasa inhaled loudly. "With both the laird and his sister gone, along with all the able-bodied men, this was Davina's chance. She must have been planning this and waiting for the opportunity."

What irony. To travel hundreds of years only to die in a horrible airless box beneath the castle. Could fate really be so cruel?

Refusing to dwell on the misery, Skye determined to keep up their spirits as long as possible. Hopefully, Ian would return soon and save them.

"Tell me about your life here," Skye encouraged. "Have you ever wed? How did you come to run the castle?"

"Aye, I was wed years ago to the love of me life. We grew up together and as soon as I started me courses, we married. It was a good match. He was a big, brute of a man who was as gentle as the lambs he tended." She drew in a breath, held it as she washed in memory, then released it. "He was killed in a raid. Ambushed. Kilt

177

seven before he went down, though." Skye sensed rather than saw the tears fall. The darkness invaded them and made the tale even more poignant.

"I am so sorry."

"Sadly, it is sometimes the way of life." She paused and swallowed. "I had a choice then. I could sink into the depths of a broken heart or find a way to keep going. My James would not have tolerated self-pity. He would have spurred me on to do something with my life. So I appealed to the laird, Ian's father, for work to keep busy and took on one task after another. The funny thing about most people is—if you'll do their work, they'll let ye."

Skye chuckled at that. "True. Where I lived before, I was never one to sit back. I worked and studied and always tried to better myself. And if I offered to take up a task, most took a step back."

"Well that means we willna just give up."

"Is there any way to escape from here we have not thought of?"

"Only a sympathetic heart or death."

***

Skye blinked awake, damp icy stones seeping into her bones. She had prayed all this was a nightmare and she would wake up in her bed, Ian by her side and Dionadair at her feet. Dionadair! She prayed Davina had not harmed the pup, but realized the woman would have to explain that to Ian. Odds were the dog was safe, if miserable. The throbbing in her arm from the wound Davina inflicted and the burning in her knees reminded her of the reality.

Neasa was wide awake, her limbs vibrating with fear and cold. "I think it's morning," she said. "I managed to doze. And I'm glad you did, too. At least the rats have stayed away."

"No food to tempt them closer?" Skye asked.

"Nay. No water either."

Most didn't drink water in the sixteenth century, opting for ale or even wine when they could get it, but even a drop of anything would be welcome.

"Three days."

"What?" Neasa asked.

"We can only live three days without water. But the freezing temperatures will take us first."

"Not a bad way to go, I suppose. I've heard ye just fall asleep."

"Well, I, for one, am not ready." Standing slowly, her limbs aching, Skye reached down to take hold of Neasa's hands. "Come on. We must move. I want to be alive when Ian returns."

It took Neasa a few moments longer to get to her feet, but then the two linked arms and paced the small square of their cell. An errant sound stopped them both in their tracks. Footsteps.

"Are they coming to execute us?" Skye asked, her fear making her vibrate.

"Nay, they dare not. At least, I think they dare not." But the quiver in her voice relayed her terror.

The footsteps came closer and stopped. "I brought bread and water," a small voice whispered.

"Freya?" Neasa asked.

"If she catches me, I will surely join you." There was no doubt Freya referred to Davina. "But I could not let you starve or die of thirst. You have both been good to me."

Freya's hands shook as she passed a flagon of water and a loaf of bread through the bars.

"You are very brave," Skye said.

"I am not. I am terrified."

"You are brave because you are here in spite of your fear," Neasa responded. "Thank ye. But go now before you are missed."

"I will come back later with blankets."

"Just be careful. And you have our deepest gratitude," Skye said.

Trying to contain her greed, Skye first offered the water to Neasa, then took small sips herself. Finally, thirst slaked for the moment, they both turned their attention to the bread.

"We must eat it all or the rats will fight us for it," Neasa declared.

Skye knew that would not be difficult. Neasa quickly divided the bounty and handed Skye her share. Knowing once hunger no longer tore at them, they would be able to concentrate on other things. Maybe even a way to escape.

"What will happen when Ian returns?" Skye asked.

"I suppose it depends. If we have died here, Davina will have to explain herself. Although she will probably accuse you of witchcraft or being a spy and trying to poison the clan women."

"But what would be my reason?"

"Davina is verra clever with words. She can make people believe even when they ken better."

"How did she come to be here. Was she born in the castle? And more, why is her behavior tolerated?"

Neasa pressed her lips together. "She was orphaned as a bairn and her relatives asked the laird, Ian's father, to take her. The old laird was a kind man and gave her to a childless couple to raise. She was a beautiful bairn and a joy when she so chose. But, if she didnae get her way, she could be a terror. Once she got what she wanted, she would be verra sorry for misbehaving and charm whoever she had wronged."

"Sounds like *The Bad Seed*." The reference slipped out and Skye hoped Neasa didn't question it by asking, so she hurriedly continued. "How did she come to be here at the castle?"

"Her mother and father died when their cottage caught fire one night. Only Davina managed to escape." Neasa hesitated a moment, as if reluctant to say more. "I'm not one to spread tales, but many suggested the fire was no accident." Neasa paused again, as if emphasizing the truth of those rumors. "Of course, when questioned, Davina was so tearful, people felt sorry for her. She was always good at that kind of thing. And she always wanted to live here. The cottage wasn't grand enough for her."

"And, since she was homeless, the old laird brought her to the castle."

"Aye. She has managed to get what she sets her mind to and any that gossip about her or try to shun her regret it. And she has convinced the menfolk she is truly innocent. Men are so easily fooled."

"But she never was able to get Ian."

"No. And she has wanted him since they were children. But he was never drawn to her. And she wouldnae accept it."

"But why is it that the other women fear her so?"

"They know what she is capable of. There have been many times when misfortune fell upon those Davina did not favor. Years ago, a young girl made her angry for some reason and when she went to tend the herb garden, she was bitten by an adder. She nearly died."

181

"And you think Davina put the snake there?"

Neasa shrugged. "It was worrisome enough to frighten all the others. That and too many accidents to be explained around the gel. I knew she was just a wee tyrant, but I could never find proof against her. I never believed her lies and I always saw through her manipulations. That's why she used this excuse to imprison me with you."

Footsteps interrupted their conversation. Not knowing who was coming to them or why, they grasped hands and held tight. Luckily, it was Freya.

Looking back down the corridor, Freya thrust some blankets between the bars and more water and bread. "The day-old bread is the best I could do," she said apologetically. "I dare not raise suspicions, although Kenna is just as worried about you as I am. We are working on plans to get you released, but with Davina in charge and neither the laird nor his sister here, it is most difficult. Hopefully, one or both will return soon."

"You are a godsend, Freya, and we are both so grateful," Skye said. "Thank you."

Freya hesitated and turned back to Skye, her eyebrows raised in question.

"What is it?" Skye asked.

"It is the lad, Rory. He has taken sick. Verra sick. With rashes and fever. And Davina has banished him to some unused stables in Dornie to die." A tear coursed down her cheek. "He is me sister's lad and she is distraught."

Skye concentrated on what she remembered from her studies. The resurgence of the Bubonic Plague apparently originated in France among the soldiers. And potatoes were available in France.

Skye gasped. "Oh my God."

Freya's eyes widened at Skye's tone. "What is it? Do ye ken."

"Aye. You must listen to me verra carefully and do everything I say. Promise."

Freya nodded almost convulsively.

"Do you ken where my bag is? The one I brought with me?"

"Davina has taken it. She is even now wearing your gown."

Lightheaded at the thought Davina might put on the cloak, Skye inhaled to calm herself. "Where is the bag itself?"

"In Davina's quarters, I believe. Tucked away under her bed. She didn't know I saw her take it and then hide it."

Skye took another deep breath. Okay. "Davina mentioned a meeting with a French soldier. She must have sent Rory to get the potatoes. That's how he came in contact with the disease."

"But how did she know the soldier would have them?"

"Maybe she didn't. It could be she sent Rory to find something, anything that would make me look guilty. It is possible that the soldier was looking to sell them. Or maybe, Davina knew they were sold in France and had Rory find someone who could get them for him. I don't know. We may never know her scheme. But it matters not now."

Both Neasa and Freya were shaking their heads now. "Davina cares not who she hurts if it means getting what she wants," Neasa said.

"I have some medicine that can make Rory well. A doctor gave it to me when my father and mother took sick. It was too late for them, but it saved me."

There was enough light to see Freya's expression was now hopeful.

"But you must be verra careful. No one can get too near him and if they do, to give him water and medicine, they must wear a cloth over their mouth and nose. If he were to cough or sneeze, others could get sick, too."

"I cannot…" Freya said, her whole body quaking with fear.

"If you listen to me, you will be safe. I promise. If you do not, Rory will likely die and others in the clan can get sick. You must be brave."

"I will try," she said, tears coursing down her cheeks.

"Find my bag. Then, slice open the fabric on the side. You will see several glass bottles. Take the one marked with a *D*."

Freya shook her head and shrugged. "I cannot read, my lady."

Skye turned to the wall and drew a *D* with her finger. "It looks like this. Can you remember?"

"Aye."

"Good." Skye nodded. "Now, Rory must swallow two pills twice a day for a sennight, two in the morning and two at night."

"Is it poison as Davina said? She warned us you might try to give us something evil." Terrified now, Freya backed away.

"Do nae be *glaikit*, girl," Neasa nearly shouted at her. "Do ye not ken the French know medicines? Our lady has been naught but good to you. How dare ye accuse her?"

Freya dropped her head in shame. "Forgive me, my lady. I should know ye would not harm us."

"I give you my oath, the medicine can only help. If he gets it in time, it will make him well. Now, repeat to me what you are to do."

"Get the medicine from yer bag, cover me face, and give Rory the *d* medicine two times a day, two pills each time, for a sennight."

"Good. Now go. And waste no time. The sooner he takes the cure, the sooner all in the clan will be safe." Freya turned away, but Skye stopped her. "One thing more. In the bag is my cloak. You must hide it where it willnae be found by another. It is important. And hide the medicine. If Davina discovers it, your fate will certainly be like ours."

Freya nodded and scurried away as Skye took to pacing, trying desperately not to think about the risks of the Bubonic Plague ravaging through the clan, Skye whispered prayers under her breath.

"Is it true, what you told Freya?" Neasa asked, her tone gentle. "Or were ye just trying to give her hope?"

"The medicine is a miracle. I have seen it work, but it must be given before the sickness has gone too far. I just hope we're in time."

"You think Rory brought this scourge upon us? Or rather Davina's intrigues?"

"I know the plague started again in France. And potatoes are eaten there and so are easily available. Davina mentioned a Frenchman and soldiers are free to travel between here and there. I only hope the man who gave them to Rory didnae make many others ill."

But Skye knew that to be a vain wish. The disease would tear through Europe again. Their only hope, since the castle was isolated, was to cure Rory and see no others had contact with French soldiers.

185

"And the cloak?" Neasa asked.

"The cloak?"

"You told her to hide yer cloak. Does it have to do with Rory being taken sick?"

The cloak. How could she explain that the time travel cloak in the wrong hands could wreak havoc on history. To say nothing of being her only way back home if things here went south. Thinking fast, she found the answer.

"It was my mother's, and it is old and torn. But it is all I have left of her. I was worried Davina would destroy it to spite me." Skye hoped the explanation would suffice.

***

Another day passed and a night and then another. The blankets were a blessing against the damp cold, but Freya had not reappeared, and thirst and hunger gnawed at the two trapped together.

Skye's wounds had indeed become contaminated in the filthy cell. Believing her knees might heal on their own, since she was healthy, she feared the cut on her arm was deeper than she first suspected and was now beginning to swell with infection. It throbbed painfully and, without soap or water, she dared not even think of the impending sepsis.

"My lady…" Neasa began.

"You must call me Skye. Especially now."

"Skye, might I ask you some questions that have gnawed at me."

"Questions?" Skye was unsure how to react. Did Neasa still doubt her loyalty? Her love for Ian? Did she wonder if Skye was a witch? She couldn't possibly think the truth. If Skye were to tell her about the cloak, Neasa would never believe her and never trust her again. But she had to know what Neasa was going to ask. Then, if she could think on her feet, she might satisfy the other woman's curiosity.

"Yes?"

"The story you told when you arrived. Now, it's not that I question your heart is good and that you truly love Ian. It's just that you know things. Like the pills for Rory."

"Yes. We had them in France."

"Did ye? Or are you secretly a healer and you did nae want to challenge me ways?"

Relief spread through Skye like a balm. "What I said was true. The pills were offered for my mother and father, but they were too far gone. The healer there told me they fight the plague if consumed early and they also help with wounds that get infected."

"As yours is?"

"How can you tell?"

"Not to be unseemly, my la—Skye—but I can smell it."

"I fear you're right. It throbs constantly now." That was truly an understatement. A thousand burning knives poking at the wound could not have hurt more.

"I have nae doubt Davina hoped this would happen. Then she wouldn't have to murder you. The wound would do it for her."

Footsteps. Even though they both hoped Freya had returned, there was the constant fear that Davina had thought of some way to rid herself of her prisoners. Both sat quietly, praying.

It was Freya's voice that cheered them. "I brought

187

ale and bread." Her whispered voice was like a hug, bringing reassurance and hope. Quickly, she passed the food through the bars. The two women had just enough time to pull the bag into their cell when they heard another's footsteps. Freya gasped.

"Hide," Skye whispered frantically.

Freya scurried down the corridor, and slipped into the dungeon beside the occupied one, as Neasa quickly grabbed the blankets from the floor and tucked them and the bag Freya had brought into the darkest corner of the cell. Hopefully, it would be in enough shadow as to be invisible.

Davina sauntered over to the cell door. Narrowing her eyes, she peered in, and a smile curved her mouth. "Hmmm. Ye do nae look so bad. Either of ye. Perhaps this life agrees with you."

"You will not get away with this, Davina," Neasa snarled.

"Aye, I will. The other women listen to me."

"Because you threaten them," Skye said, through her teeth.

Davina shrugged. "No one has come down here for years. The other women believe angry spirits cry out in the cells and wish to harm anyone who dares walk here. And there is no doubt among them that I have saved them from a witch." Grinning, she shrugged. "The laird will never even think to search when he is told you have left to find the queen."

"He will not believe you." Skye retorted with more confidence than she felt.

"Aye, he will. And with the others to agree, he will nae challenge me. Trust me, none of the women will dare tell him where you are. If any did have a change of heart and would dare risk telling him the truth, I will see to it they have no chance to get near enough." She grinned and it was an ugly sight. "And I will offer him the comfort he needs after his miserable wife deserted him."

Skye was vibrating with rage. "And how will you explain Neasa being gone?"

Davina turned her gaze on the older woman. "She is not as loved as she thinks. When I tell Ian she left to find you and try to convince you to return, he will believe me."

"And when I never return?" Neasa asked.

Davina shrugged. "So much can happen. Why our lady here was set upon, was she nae? If that part of her tale is even true." Davina smirked. "And how is your arm, my lady? I have nae doubt it pains you greatly. Soon, I am certain it will be the death of you." Davina huffed. "Well, I must be away. The laird should return soon, and I must prepare."

She stepped back and giggled, then swept down the corridor and out of sight.

"Will Ian believe her?" Skye asked, the thought terrifying. "If he does, we will surely die down here." Tears filled her eyes and spilled down her cheeks. "I love him so. And he will not ever know I would never desert him."

"Ye must have faith," Neasa said. "It is all we can hope for."

Skye's knees gave way and she sank to the hard, cold, damp floor. She dare not tell Neasa the whole truth, but would it matter now? They were destined to die in this cold, dark miserable cell while the love of her life believed she had left him.

"What if you wrote him a note?" Neasa suggested. "When you hear of his return, send him a missive, telling him we are here."

189

Skye brightened. "Yes. Of course! We could get Freya to give it to him or Conall. Skye stood and hugged the other woman, the burning pain in her arms easing a little with this bit of hope.

Freya emerged from the shadows, smiling. "What she said is true. Many are terrified by Davina's threats. She has many convinced she has the power to ruin them and take away all that they value in this world."

Skye knew the power of a bully. Cowards at heart, they nevertheless could convince others to go along with the most heinous acts. If only she had the chance to intervene.

"Then you have even more courage than I imagined," Skye said.

"You saved one who means a great deal to me. It slipped me mind, but thanks to you, Rory is recovering. And since no one else has gone near him but me, no one else is ill. And you can see I am sound. I will never forget what you did by giving me the pills."

Skye exhaled her relief at this news. The plague would not tear through the castle now and leave it devastated.

"The pills," Neasa said, stepping closer to the bars. "Are there any remaining?"

"Aye. Enough for the remaining days and more besides."

"Good. Bring the rest of the medicine down here as soon as you can. The Lady Skye needs them."

Freya opened her mouth in horror. "My Lady?"

"No," Skye objected. "I only have what is in the bottle and when that is gone, there is no more. I cannot take the medicine in case someone else gets sick and needs it."

"You will take it," Neasa said, iron in her tone. "You will be no good to us dead. I will brook no disagreement here." She turned to Freya. "Save aside enough for Rory and bring the rest.

"And something to write with. Can ye do that?"

Freya nodded and was gone.

Later, the sound of footfalls returning had them both on edge. It could be Davina returning to gloat—or maybe Freya coming back. But the steps sounded different. Who came now to add to their torment?

When Kenna came into view, both Skye and Neasa breathed huge sighs of relief. She leaned against the cell and pushed a basket through the bars. "Bread, cheese, and ale," she whispered.

"Thank you. Bless you," Skye said, her heart bursting, knowing the Kenna risked much to be here.

"I meant to come sooner, but Davina and her minions watch constantly. We were told that anyone who offered you aid would join you. And the others are very frightened. Davina has them convinced she has the power to kill their children. And she has promised that when the laird returns, she will be his wife. And then any who defied her will pay dearly."

"We thank you for your courage," Skye said. "But I must know, Kenna. How did ye know I was innocent? You did nae join the others in bringing us down here."

Kenna smiled. "Truth be told, the potatoes terrified me, but I could nae believe you would harm us. You love Laird Ian, it is clear to anyone with eyes. And you are his wife. Why would you choose to hurt us? It made nae sense to me. And—Davina is eaten by her jealousy and ambition. To believe her accusations would be to play the fool."

"I am so glad," Skye said.

"I wish I could do more to see to yer release, but I dare not until the laird's return. He alone can save you now. I must go before I am missed." And she rushed back down the dark corridor.

***

Another day had passed. Skye could barely sit up. The chill in her bones caused her to shiver uncontrollably and her upper arm was on fire.

"You are burning up," Neasa said, tears in her voice. "I've been praying Freya will return, but what if she has been caught?"

Through chattering lips, Skye managed a smile. "If she had been caught, she would be here with us. I have to believe she is safe and will return soon."

"She had best hurry or Davina will not have to do more to see your life ended."

As if in answer to a prayer, the next morning Freya appeared at the cell and thrust the small bottle of pills between the bars.

Skye was huddled on the floor, her body rocked with tremors. Clearly sick with worry, Neasa grabbed the bottle Freya had brought and knelt beside Skye.

"Is she…?" Freya voice broke before she could ask.

"Alive but taken by the fever. I pray this medicine will do its work and quickly." She looked back over her shoulder at Freya. "Go, before you are seen. And pray. Pray for all you're worth."

"I also brought a piece of linen rag and some charcoal for writing, just as you asked."

Freya thrust the items through the bars and scurried away.

Neasa again turned to Skye.

"Ye must get well, my lady. We cannot lose you."

But Skye didn't hear her words. Dreams had taken her, and she was in a nightmarish landscape, cold and bleak. Someone was shoving something in her mouth. She nearly choked but managed to swallow the awful tasting potion that was pushed between her lips. And then she was wandering again.

In the distance, Ian waited for her. But he was slipping away.

She reached out to him. "Come back to me. Do not leave me here alone."

Chapter Eighteen

There was naught better than coming home to the clan after a victory. And this time, Ian had a beautiful wife waiting to greet him. He imagined his homecoming would be filled with as many hours as he and Skye could manage alone together. The delights of exploring each other's bodies made his groin tighten in anticipation.

He had also invited his fellow Belligerents to Eilean Donan for some Highland games to celebrate their victory. Although the games usually concluded no later than September, this was a special occasion. Looking forward to dancing with his lady and showing off the skills of his clan made this homecoming even more pleasurable.

Errol rode up beside him, grinning. "Which is better, brother? Winning this last battle or coming home to your beautiful bride?"

"Aye, ye read me mind. And do nae forget the upcoming games."

"We will best the other clans, I hae no doubt."

"I suppose you are anxious to see your wife, as well."

"I never thought a woman would steal me heart, but your sister is…"

"Special?" Ian finished the sentence.

"More than special. She is all to me. You know that."

"I do, which is why I agreed to let you marry her."

"As if you could tell her what to do."

"She can be single-minded. She gets that from me."

"Nae a doubt."

"And how goes it with your bride?"

"If I said she was the sun and moon to me, you might think I had gone daft."

They both laughed as Conall came up beside them, his expression sheepish. "I hae a confession, Laird."

Ian raised an eyebrow. He hated to be distracted from talk of his bride, but he did have an obligation to hear what Conall needed to say. "Aye, do ye now? Well, out with it, mon."

"Do I need to go?" Errol asked.

"Nay. There are no secrets among us."

"Go on," Ian urged.

"I've been thinking on the subject and I believe I've changed me mind."

"Aboot?"

"Well, if you recall, I said I wished to pursue Davina, she of the large endowments."

Ian chuckled at this.

"Hae you laid eyes on Freya—before we left?" Conall's eyes were wide.

Grinning, Ian stroked his chin. "Aye. There have been some changes. For the better."

"It seems your bride has had an influence."

"Are ye saying ye've changed your mind aboot the woman you wish to pursue."

"I think I have."

"She is a quiet little thing."

195

"And since when is a quiet woman not a good thing?" He responded, sounding slightly defensive.

Ian held up both hands in a surrendering gesture, then reached again for his reins. "Nay, not a bad thing. And she is sweet enough."

Conall was silent for a moment. "Is it me, or do ye think Davina is a bit mean spirited?"

Ian shook his head. "No question. But now I find meself in a bit of a quandary."

"I understand not."

"Well, with you taking up Davina's time, I was hoping she'd set her sights in your direction. If you choose Freya instead, I may have to find her a mate to keep her from her games."

"Do ye think it was she that put the thorn under Morel's saddle?"

"Let's just say I wouldnae be surprised. Though she would nae do it herself. More that another would do such a thing to please her."

"Davina has lusted for you for a long time, Ian. It would serve her if the lady were hurt or killed."

Ian shuddered at that thought. "It would nae. There was always something aboot her that put me off, long before Skye, so there was naught a chance she would ever be my wife."

"I sense it, too." Conall hesitated. "Why did you nae warn me, then, when I said I wished to pursue her."

"It isnae up to me what attracts another mon. I didnae think she was dangerous, and I had faith you could handle her. But I am much relieved you have set your sights in another direction."

The castle loomed ahead, and the men spurred their horses onward in anticipation.

As they reached the stables, Ian was suddenly aware of Dionadair barking in the distance. The sound carried across the loch and Ian smiled. So, the dug missed him and was anxious for his return. He had no doubt his mistress felt the same and Ian could not wait to hold her again.

But where was his mistress? Since she arrived, if the dug was not with him, he was with Skye.

As he listened more closely, there was something in the pup's bark that sounded strange. A frisson of apprehension traveled up Ian's spine and he leapt off his horse, throwing his reins to a waiting stableboy.

"Ian?" Errol called out. "What's amiss?"

"Errol, Conall, Daimh, hurry. To the castle." With that, he jumped into a waiting boat and was immediately followed by the others.

The closer they got to the shore, the more the feeling of dread caused Ian's heart to race. And, he had no sooner touched solid ground than the pup increased his cries, turning in furious circles, and howling with what sounded to Ian like distress.

Ian knelt down and reached out to the pup to calm him, but Dionadair would have none of it. He was limping and Ian lifted one of the dog's paws. It was raw and bleeding. "Have you been lost?" Ian asked.

Ian turned to the other men. "Dionadair has been out of the castle for what appears to be days. Something is verra wrong." Picking up the dog and cradling him, Ian raced up the embankment, followed by the other three.

Bursting into the main hall, Ian's voice rang out. "Why has Dionadair been sent outside?" Ian demanded. His gaze swept the space. The other women present pressed against the walls, looking terrified. "What has happened in our absence?" Desperate to remain calm so he could think, Ian instinctively reached for his dagger. "And where is the Lady Skye?" Ice cold filled his veins, and he gritted his teeth, ready to exact revenge on anyone who had dared harm her.

Stepping forward, Davina swiped at her eyes as if she had been crying. "Forgive me, Laird, for being the bearer of such bad tidings. But your wife—has left ye." Bowing her head, she took a step forward, reaching out to him.

Ignoring her gesture, he glared at her. "What?" Her words made no sense.

"Left me? To go where?" A thousand possibilities skittered through his mind, but none were logical.

"To the queen. It seems she missed the life at court after all." Davina shook her head and pressed her lips together.

Ian frowned at her in utter disbelief. "Nay. You jest." He moved back. "Neasa?" he called out.

When the older woman did not appear, he tried again. "Neasa?" This time he was louder.

Again, Davina spoke, taking the opportunity to move closer still. "Gone, too, Laird. I suppose the lady took this opportunity to go, since you were nae here to allay her."

Now Ian was really confused. None of Davina's words made sense. "Explain what occurred in my absence and why my dug was left outside to fend for himself. Was he trying to leave, too?" It all sounded ridiculous.

Davina inhaled, as if preparing to deliver the most hateful of news. "Neasa went after your wife, hoping to convince her to return. Or, mayhap she was tired of all the work and responsibility after all these years. We have not heard from either of them since they left, have we?"

Turning to face the women pressing against the walls, she silently demanded agreement. Several of the others merely nodded.

Gently, Ian laid the pup on a bench, and sank down next to him. He was frozen, unable to think or react. His heart was shattered and still the damnable thing kept beating.

Davina eased herself down next to him. "Laird?"

"Get away from me," he growled. "Somehow I believe you are behind this."

Davina gasped. "Laird. How can ye say such a thing. I have ne'er sought to do anything but see to yer happiness."

Suddenly, he stood and straightened his spine. His battle cry resounded through the hall. Grabbing anything he could lay his hands on, he flung mugs and vessels and bowls against the walls, his fury unabated by his actions. The women ran from the room as if chased by the devil himself. Only Davina remained quietly and waiting for the storm to pass.

Finally, winded with his exertions, Ian stomped back over the bench where Dionadair sat, picked up the pup and sank into a chair by the fire. "Ale. Bring me ale."

Davina hastened to do as he asked.

***

Pain permeated Skye's dreams as fire tore through her arm. Crying out, it took but a moment before sweet relief replaced the agony. A sickening smell filled the air, and she was being pulled backward. Something slipped into her mouth and she gagged but managed to swallow. A sip of ale eased the desert of her throat, and then she was thrust into the dreamscape again. This time it was not so cold, and inhaling was not such a trial.

Time lost all meaning and all that remained was darkness and light, fighting to wake, slipping into oblivion. Slowly, after hours, days, Skye had no idea, she blinked awake. The floor beneath her was hard and damp and the odor was much worse than she remembered. But above her was Neasa's face, smiling.

"Welcome back, Skye."

"I was away?" Confusion made everything misty, and her voice was a croak, rattling in her throat.

"Ye almost left me for the land beyond. Ye have been terrible sick."

Trying to raise her right arm was still a trial and she vaguely remembered worse pain. "Tell me."

"The wound indeed festered and swelled. The cut Davina gave you. I gave you the pills, but it wasnae enough. So, I found a sharp-edged stone and punctured it." Neasa smiled. "Nasty stuff poured forth, but it seems the poison came out and you started the climb back."

The memories seeped back. Gingerly, Skye touched the wound. It was sticky and damp, but not throbbing as it had. "You saved me."

"Aye. From that wound. But we still linger here, abandoned and forgotten. Neither Freya nor Kenna have visited for a day, and I fear we shall not survive."

"But Ian must have returned by now. He will look for us."

"No. He would have no reason. It is as Davina said. She will spread her lies and he will have no cause to doubt her."

Tears slipped down Skye's cheeks, the total misery threatened to envelop her. Pressing her lips together, she determined not to lose hope. Not until her last breath.

"Did I remember Freya brought some linen and an instrument to write? Or did I dream it?

"Nay, it wasnae a dream. It is here."

Neasa handed Skye the bit of cloth and the charcoal. Her pulse increasing with hope, Skye realized her hand shook as she tried to write. She must keep it simple, so she wrote a single word. "When Freya returns, we must make certain to give this to her. She must get it to Ian."

As if by magic, small footsteps echoed down the corridor. By now, the two recognized Freya's steps. Joy lightened Skye's heart. Freya would see that Ian received the note and he would come.

"I hae only a moment," Freya whispered as she reached the bars. "The laird has returned but Davina has convinced him you both deserted him while he fought for the queen. He is roaring with fury, and I fear Davina has accomplished her purpose."

"Take this," Skye said, thrusting the note to the other woman. "See that it reaches Ian."

Davina watches him like a hawk. She will ne'er let me near enough to him."

"Then give it to Conall," Skye said. Knowing very few of the clan could read, Davina would not suspect a note would be given to any but Ian himself. It was their only hope.

Stuffing the missive into a pocket of her gown, Freya disappeared up the hallway.

"And now we pray," said Neasa.

Both sinking down to the cold stones, they leaned against the wall. All they could do now is wait.

After a while, Neasa broke the silence.

"A strange thing happened when ye were in the throes. Yer *Francach* accent was no more. Ye spoke of

201

yer love for Ian, one named Harper, and oddly, yer brogue was not in evidence, either."

"Oh," was all Skye could respond. The situation was now dire, but all she could hear in her head was Ricky Ricardo telling Lucy she had "some splaining to do."

"Ye have no reason not to tell me all, now," Neasa encouraged. "I know yer nae a spy and I am certain you love Ian. But mayhap how you came to us has not been truly told."

"You deserve the truth, but I have no doubt you will not believe it."

***

Mug after mug of ale did not lessen Ian's misery. It only made him want to piss. Holding on to Dionadair, he refused to release the pup even though he squirmed and whimpered.

Davina's hovering did not help, and he ordered her away to be left alone in his agony.

He had loved Skye, with his verra soul. She had said she loved him in return, only to leave him with no explanation. Why? Why? He would hae given her anything she asked. The world. Could she not wait until his return so they could talk? Wummin! He hated them all. And her most of all!

Errol crept up to him, clearly reluctant.

"What?" Ian demanded. "Can ye not leave me be and let me die?"

"Forgive me, Ian, but I have been told Maisie has gone to Kintail to tend her cousin Claray. I'll not be satisfied until I see her with me own eyes. I hate leaving you in this state, but I must fetch her, and I know it will help if she is here with you now."

His words sank in, and Ian nodded. "Go. See that my sister is safe. And the bairn. Bring her home."

Daimh and Conall appeared on either side of Ian as Errol hurried away.

"Come on, Laird. Time for bed," Conall said.

Ian turned his head to the other man. "Why?"

"Come with us. Sleep," Daimh urged.

Conall spoke up now. "There has to be more to the tale we havenae been told. The lady loves you. It is in her eyes each time she looks at ye. Take heart, we shall get to the bottom of this."

"She didnae just leave, did she? It makes no sense," Ian responded.

"Sleep now," Daimh encouraged. "We shall solve this mystery come the morning."

As Ian tried to stand, Dionadair slipped to the floor. Whimpering and barking, he raced to the far alcove and twisted in circles.

"I miss her, too, pup, but it's possible she isnae coming back." Sadness so pervasive made him feel sick. Ian patted his side to call the dog, but Dionadair kept up his frantic yelping.

"Get me dug," Ian instructed Conall. "I'm to bed."

***

"… And when I saw his portrait, I knew he was the man I was to love. I had to find him."

"So ye came through time? Through the Druid stones?" Neasa was shaking her head, clearly trying to understand. "I have heard of such things, but they are only tales passed down. Are ye saying it is possible?"

Skye knew the concept of Ebay would be too much,

so she left that part out. "I found an old cloak that was supposed to have the power. I wrapped myself in it and when I woke up, I was in the cottage where you first found me." Skye's hand flew to her mouth. "The cloak. I pray Davina has not found it." She could only imagine if one like Davina traveled forward in time.

"Yer saying a piece of cloth has that power?"

"I know. I really thought it was impossible, but you can see it worked. But it had to. I was so in love with Ian from the beginning, I had to find him, no matter what it took."

"And the tale about the queen?" Neasa pressed her lips together, stifling a grin.

"I had to explain how I came to be here. I could not let you think I was a spy or had evil intent."

Neasa was shaking her head. "I know not of such things as the truth of folklore, but I do know the power of love. And that much I believe." She hesitated a moment. "Are ye certain the fever doesnae still have a hold on ye?"

Skye nodded. "I am sure." A cloak with that kind of power was more than difficult to believe. If she were Neasa, belief would be challenging, especially in a time when such things were only —fairy tales.

"I do find this hard to swallow. How is it even possible? Tell me something to convince me."

"Like what?" Thinking for a moment, Skye pulled off her shoe and held her foot up to the sparse light. The nail polish was chipped, but still visible. "Does this persuade you?"

"What is it on yer toes?"

"It's like a varnish. Very common practice for women in my time."

"What is it like? Where you come from? Is it so different?"

204

"Very! And it was actually one of your relatives that encouraged me. A MacKenzie. And yes, my time is different in some ways, but people are basically the same. Some are good, some are not. It is the way of things." Skye shifted her position, wondering what she could say that would make sense. "I think many would like to be able to go to the past or to the future. They just need a—carriage of sorts. It's hard for me to explain since I really don't understand it myself. All I know is that I had to come here, to meet Ian, to love him face-to-face. My best friend believed I had lost my mind, and I can't tell her anything different. But I am here and even if we never see the light of day again, it was all worth it to spend the hours I did with the man I love."

Neasa shook her head. "It is not so easy to accept, but I suppose life holds many mysteries we will ne'er understand."

"So ye believe me?"

"It would explain some of the words ye use. And yer accent."

"It's American. But that's a place that won't come into being for a long while yet."

"T'is much to take in. Does Ian know the truth?"

"No. I tried to tell him, but I was afraid he would think I was daft. Or a witch."

Neasa nodded. "Aye, I can see that." Neasa patted her arm. "When he rescues us, I will keep yer secret. It is not mine to tell."

"Thank you. You are a good friend."

Suddenly, exhaustion washed through Skye, and she leaned back against the wall. "I am so tired."

"Sleep now. And we will pray help comes on the morrow."

***

Hands were stroking his legs, soft lips caressing his neck. It felt wonderful. Half asleep, Ian didn't fight to waken. Fingers tightened around his manhood, hard now and aching for release. "Skye? Ye came back."

"No, Ian, she is gone forever, but I am here."

Opening his eyes, it was Davina, naked, who hovered above him, her long hair sweeping his chest. Jumping up, he nearly sent her toppling to the floor. "Are ye mad? Get out of me bed."

"But, Ian," she wheedled. "I am here and willing. Yer faithless wife has gone away, but I am ever loyal. Am I no consolation?"

"Nae. Go!" Fury enveloped him. Maybe Skye had been faithless, but he could not so easily forget her and move on.

Before she could move, the door to his chamber slammed against the wall, causing both Ian and Davina to jump. "Laird!" It was Daimh, with Conall behind him.

The men stopped, their mouths agape as Davina grabbed her gown and stood.

"What now?" Ian demanded, sitting up and shaking his head. "And whatever it is, remove this woman from my sight."

Daimh moved toward her as Conall held out a bit of linen to Ian. "I told ye. I told ye," he repeated. "Freya said to bring this to ye without delay! It is from your lady!"

"What does it say?" Ian jumped up, his full attention on the other men. Remembering neither man could read, Ian reached for the scrap of cloth, but when he went to grasp it, Davina leaped forward and tore it away, pulling it into her fist.

"Give me that!" Ian spat at her, stalking toward her as she backed against the wall.

"Nay. It is some falsehood. I just ken it." Davina bit her lower lip, her attempt to look pathetic very unconvincing.

"I hae never struck a wummin before, but if you do nae show me that paper, it will be a first." Ian's voice was quiet, but the menace in it was unmistakable.

"Ye cannot believe it." Tears now rolled down her cheeks.

"How can ye know what it says? Give it over."

Reluctantly, she stretched out her hand and dropped the note, then hurried from the room.

Bending to open it, it said one word in a shaky hand. "*Dungeon.*"

Ian grabbed his tartan and raced from the room. "Follow me. Now!"

Chapter Nineteen

Dionadair still stood guard at the door behind the main hall as Ian ran down the steps. Seeing his master, he jumped up, barking and crying.

"Good boy." Ian patted him, then yanked on the heavy portal, forcing it wide. "The dug was trying to tell me and I was too daft to pay heed."

Daimh and Conall were clearly confused but waited to follow Ian's lead. Rushing down the stone steps into the darkness, Ian called out into the void. "I'm coming."

Grabbing a torch from the wall, he thrust it at Daimh. The other man grabbed it and rushed to the fire to light the thing, then thrust it back to Ian. Together the three stomped down the slippery steps and into the dim corridor. Dionadair was on their heels as they made their way down the passageway.

Nothing prepared Ian for the sight in the first cell. A roar tore from his throat and echoed off the dark walls. Rage wrapped its iron fingers around his chest, making it difficult to breath. Taking a moment to collect himself, he was able to speak. "Skye, my love. And Neasa. How did this happen?"

"Ian, I knew you'd come. See, Neasa, we had faith!" Tears poured down her cheeks as she reached for Neasa, and they held onto each other. "We are saved." She faced her husband. "Oh, Ian, I love you so. I knew you would not believe her."

Dionadair was yipping and jumping toward the iron bars. "I worried so when they put you out, little pup," Skye whispered, leaning down to pet the dog, new tears running down her cheeks.

"Find the key," he demanded of Conall as he reached through the bars to touch his much-abused wife. No words came to him as he surveyed the scene. The two women had been thrust here for God knew how long. The stench alone reached into his throat, threatening to make him retch.

"Who?" he asked, his fury nearly choking him. "Who did this?"

Neasa stepped to the bars. "Davina," she whispered.

"I will kill her," he seethed. He was furious with himself for believing what Davina had told him. He knew better, but the thought of losing Skye had dulled his logic.

Conall returned carrying three axes. "The others say the key is about Davina's neck. I couldnae find her, so I chose these instead." He thrust one of the weapons toward Ian and the other to Daimh.

"Step back," he said to the women. As soon as they were against the back wall, the men took turns hacking away at the stones holding the bars. It took some time, but finally the door gave way and Skye rushed forward into Ian's arms.

She winced as he pulled her against him. "Are you hurt?"

Neasa spoke up. "She nearly died from the festering of her arm. Davina cut her with a blade."

"I will kill her," Ian repeated. "And any who aided her." Inhaling to control his fury, he placed his arm

209

around Skye and helped her along the corridor to the steps. "I want this place cleaned and then I wish to see the entrance locked tight. This damnable place is never to be breached by a clan member of mine again."

Dionadair was jumping up, desperate for her attention. Still weak from the infection, she bent down slowly, joy filling her heart. The dog jumped into her arms. "I was so worried. I know they did not treat you well and I hope you forgive me."

The pup nearly soaked her face with his furious licking. Smiling broadly, she stood and pressed herself against her husband, who carefully wrapped his arms around her and led them down the darkened corridor and up the steps. As Skye pressed against him, he could feel her loss of weight and it fueled his anger further. His wife and his dug had been cast into the most horrible of fates, Left for dead. And it was his own clanswomen, people he protected that swore fealty to him, that were responsible. And Davina—willing to murder to achieve her own ends... unforgivable. He swore an oath that he would see this righted.

As they reappeared in the main hall, several of the women gasped. One named Alba and another named Sorcha immediately fell to their knees, their hands clasped as if in prayer. "Forgive us, my lady. She made us agree," cried Sorcha.

Glaring at her, Ian pulled his dagger from its sheath and prepared to strike both women.

"She threatened my bairns," Sorcha sobbed, "and told us the Lady Skye was trying to kill us all."

Skye placed a staying hand on Ian's arm. "I do not blame the women."

"Then ye have a kinder heart than I," he said through

gritted teeth. He turned to the women. "Bring bathing tubs for my wife and Neasa and be quick. Find them both clean gowns. And food. And drink. And when they are refreshed, I will hear all that transpired and judgment will be as merciless as the treatment my lady and Neasa received."

***

Slowly, Skye and Neasa climbed the stairs to the master chamber. Tubs had already been brought and women scurried about filling them with hot water and laying out clean gowns. Neasa had Kenna bring her basket of healing herbs and, after carefully washing Skye's injured arm, bound it with clean cloths. Dionadair sat as close to Skye as he could possibly get, watching everything all at once. It was clear he had no intention of letting her out of his sight.

Since Freya had told Skye that Davina had taken her gowns and bag, she asked that her things be returned to her. It took little time before the gowns were brought to her, but her cloak was noticeably missing. Forcing herself to concentrate on ridding herself of the terrible reek of the last days, she tried to remain calm. But Neasa noticed.

"What is it?" Neasa asked.

"The cloak is gone."

Neasa's eyes widened and she pressed her fingers to her lips. "Do ye think Davina has it?"

"I know not, but it does me no good to fash," Skye whispered. "She cannot know about its abilities. I will find it." Skye sounded more confident than she felt. If Davina put the cloak on, she would be sent forward into Skye's time. Skye could not imagine the result.

Working to quell her worry, she and Neasa both sank into the soothing hot water of adjacent tubs and soaked away the filth that covered them. A table was brought and set between the two vessels and covered with breads and cakes and mugs of ale.

Sighing with relief, they scrubbed and washed their hair, and ate and drank, savoring every morsel, knowing that finally they were safe. And clean, the stench of the prison no longer clinging to their skin. But Skye was troubled with the loss of the cloak. Not that she had any intention of using it to return to her own time. It was what she feared would happen if Davina discovered its power. Telling herself that was unlikely, since the garment looked old and worth little, she hoped Davina had merely discarded it. But she would feel better if she knew what had happened to it.

Skye asked that Freya be summoned, and the other woman appeared a few moments later. "First, we wish to thank ye again for all ye did. You saved so many lives and I promise you will be rewarded."

"My lady, I have nae wish for aught. I am just so grateful you did not succumb in that terrible place."

"Freya, did ye find my cloak?"

"Nay, but I have set some of the women to keep looking. Do not fash. We will find it." Her words echoed Skye's earlier and Skye hoped they were both right.

***

As Freya returned to the main hall, Ian motioned for her to move to a corner away from the others who were gathering. Color drained from her cheeks and her eyes widened in fear.

Conall stepped up beside her and placed his hand on the small of her back. Leaning in, he whispered, "The laird only wishes to know details. He kens that you did naught but help and bringing the note saved his bride and Neasa." His hand moved up and down her back, soothing her.

"What he says is true," Ian said. "I owe you a debt of gratitude I cannot hope to repay."

"I wish I could hae done more," she responded.

"Tell me what happened, from the beginning. Leave naught out."

"... Kenna helped, as well. She made certain I was nae missed when I went to the dungeon and she herself went there with food and drink," Freya finished.

"Bring Kenna here and the two of you sit over there." He indicated a bench separated from the tables. "You are the innocents and the saviors here and I will not have anyone think otherwise."

***

A while later Skye and Neasa dressed and together walked down the stone steps to the main hall. Most of the clan was crowded into the room, anxious to witness the proceedings.

Ian had separated the three women who had participated in imprisoning her and Neasa and he was now pacing in front of them, his jaw clenched. Davina was noticeably absent. As Skye and Neasa approached, the dog at their heels, it was as if the entire group held its collective breath while the three looked up, then dropped their gazes, their shame reflected in their stances.

Off to the side, Freya and Kenna sat quietly, watching. Ian turned and spread his arms, offering a bow.

213

"My lady and Neasa, I have heard the details of the terrible, unforgivable wrongs done to you. You see before you those that condemned you. What say you?"

Skye and Neasa exchanged a look and Skye stepped forward. Before she could speak, Alba raced forward and fell to the ground, her hands clasped over her head as if in prayer. "Mercy, my lady. Mercy, we beg you."

Sorcha immediately joined the other woman on the stone floor, followed by Isla.

"Mercy," they each cried.

Sorcha lifted her head. "We made a terrible mistake. We believed Davina about the potatoes, and she threatened us, our bairns, and our families. She said when our lady and Neasa were gone, she would rule here, and we would pay for any betrayal."

Isla glanced over at Dionadair, who bared his teeth. Obviously, the pup held a grudge. "I put out food for the dug and water. I hated locking him out, but Davina insisted," she cried in her defense. Looking back to Skye, tears rolled down her cheeks. "Please, my lady. We believed her. She convinced us ye were trying to poison the clan."

"And did it nae occur to ye to wonder why I would have reason to do this?" Skye asked quietly.

It was Alba that responded. "Aye. She told us you were in league with the MacDonalds. That you had nae come from France, but instead had been sent by them and now were consorting with our enemies. And we were terrible afraid. She had us believe the MacDonald was going to attack unless we held you hostage. We thought we were saving the clan."

"Does that make sense, Alba? Did ye think to defend this castle by locking us away?"

Alba and the other two shook their heads. "We were not thinking. No, it makes no sense. But Davina had us convinced. We never should have listened to her."

Looking over to Ian, Skye sighed and shrugged. How could she exact a punishment from women who honestly thought they were showing loyalty.

Silence descended on the hall, and Skye moved closer to Ian. In a few short weeks, she had gone from being a simple apartment manager studying history, to one actually deciding it, ruling on the fate of others. No matter what she had suffered, standing as judge now was overwhelming. "A word, my lord."

Separating themselves from the group, Skye motioned for Neasa to join them. "I think I speak for Neasa when I say I cannot blame them." Ian opened his mouth, ready to protest, when she held up her hand. "Davina convinced them. And they hae only known me for a short time. I can understand why they would accept her words as truth."

Neasa shook her head. "All three have known me all their lives. Your argument does not stand, my lady."

"Would you condemn them to the same fate?" Ian asked Neasa.

Neasa blew out a breath. "Nay. I would nae do that to the lowliest of creatures. But they must be punished." Turning to Skye, she angled her head. "Do ye not see that, my lady."

"Aye. But the weight of the consequences should land on Davina. Has she been found?"

"Nay. She continues to elude those who search for her. As for the others, it must be determined the method of punishment. And how severe." His nostrils flared. "I would choose to have them drawn and quartered."

Skye pressed her lips together. "You are laird. It is up to you. But I believe the three realize the folly of their actions and, by granting mercy, we can ensure they will be more careful in future before ever condemning another."

"I would vote at least for a walk of shame," Neasa said. "But I see the wisdom of your words, my lady."

Skye leaned close to her. "Neasa, we are long past that formality. My name is Skye."

Neasa smiled and squeezed Skye's hand. "Aye, we nearly died together. We are bound tight."

Ian strode back to the women, the collective breath of those along the walls held in anticipation. Facing the members of the clan present, he held up his hand for silence. "My lady has counseled mercy and, although I would choose to be less lenient, she and Neasa were the ones who suffered. But, if you choose to shun these three, at least for a time, it would not be considered unfair. In fact, it would be proper." Ian suddenly smiled. "Better yet, you three are to scrub the cell until it smells like the first breath of spring. All the cells down there. And the hall as well. So ye will get a taste of what my lady and Neasa were subjected to. When that is done, we shall determine if your debt has been paid."

Isla ran over and fell at Skye's feet, grabbing the hem of her gown and kissing it. The other two doubled over in loud sobbing, tears washing down their faces and into the rushes.

It was then that Rory came racing into the hall, pale and breathless. He dropped to his knees at Ian's feet, panting. "Laird, my lady, it was all me fault. Davina sent me to meet the *Francach* soldier, and he gave me those brown things. She told me the lady Skye had requested them and, even though she feared they were poison, she could not go against her lady's wishes."

Gasps went up among the clan.

"No, no," Rory shouted out. "Davina lied."

Calmly, Ian lifted him to his feet. "Tell all present how you ken this."

"I knew she was lying, since she had not been at the castle for two days. She had no chance to get orders from my lady. I dared not question her—she promised me favors—and I was a fool. I did nae know what the soldier had until I returned." Shaking his head, he continued. "The *Francach* gave me more than potatoes. He gave me the Black Death. I still bear the marks." Opening his shirt, tracings of the telltale buboes marred his skin.

At his words, the men and women cried out in terror as one. "No, no," Rory yelled about the noise. "It is safe here now. It was Lady Skye who saved me, saved us. Freya brought me medicine, sent from our lady, and it fought the sickness. And my lady explained to her I was to be kept away from clan, so I would not spread death to others. Freya herself covered her face, as my lady instructed, so she would not fall ill." Rory stopped for a moment to catch his breath.

Embarrassed by all of Rory's praise, and a little apprehensive that it might arouse suspicions about her, Skye sidled closer to Ian. Stroking her hair, he smiled.

"Even with yer own life at risk, you thought to save the clan. Ye are indeed worthy to stand at me side. I hae ne'er been so proud." This was said loud enough for all to hear.

"But before that, when Davina thought I was dying, she banished me to the empty part of the stables in Dornie and then came to visit so she could laugh at me. 'Now

217

you can never say who sent you for the poison, can ye,' she told me. "Ye will die, and I will be well rid of you."

He dropped his head in shame. "I was a fool," he repeated. "And it nearly cost my life and the lives of my family."

A group of clansmen suddenly threw open the door and strode into the hall from the outside. "There is no sign of her, Laird. We have searched high and low, but she is well gone."

Ian moved to the front of the room so he could be seen by all. "Hear this. Davina is now an enemy of this clan. She not only threatened the life of my lady and Neasa, but she brought pestilence into this castle, all because her desires were not met. On her, I will show no mercy. If she is found, bring her to me. But understand, I care not if she is dead or alive."

All nodded their assent and began to file out of the hall. As they passed Skye and Neasa, they bowed and offered kind words.

Finally, all that remained were Ian, Skye, Neasa, Conall, and Daimh.

"You both must be exhausted," Ian addressed the two women.

"I am, but more I am grateful," Skye replied, Neasa nodding her agreement.

"And to think I desired to pursue that demon," Conall said, sadness in his tone.

"How could you know what lengths she would go to gain her selfish ends?" Ian asked. "Ye cannot blame yerself in this. And ye would not be the first man to be blinded by the wares a woman can display." Ian patted him on the back. "But I take it your attention has been drawn to Freya now."

"Aye. If not for her, your lady and Neasa might still be lingering in that hole of hell."

"We owe her a great debt," Skye said. "She and Kenna both risked themselves to bring us food and drink and blankets. I would like to see them rewarded."

"Yes!" Neasa agreed.

Ian nodded once. "Then we should decide what that is to be. For now, I say we get some rest and, at the rising of the sun, we find Davina. And see to her punishment as well."

Taking Skye's hand and tucking it into the crook of his elbow, Ian led her up the steps to their chamber. "So many of the clans came together in the fight at Corrichie, I had planned for some games here to celebrate our victory for our queen in two weeks' time. Do ye think ye will be up to it?"

Skye grinned. "I wouldnae miss it for the world."

***

Reaching out and stroking the line of her jaw, he marveled at how beautiful and strong this woman was. And how she held his heart in her small hands. Inhaling, he tried to control the rage that caused his fists to clench and his heart to slam into his chest. Stepping away from her, he shook his head. Guilt was eating him alive. If he had not left her unprotected... He had given his word to keep her safe. He deserted her and she was nearly taken from him. It was almost too much to bear.

"Ian. What is it?"

"The fault is mine. I brought this on you. You might have died." His voice cracked at the last.

"How can you say that? It was Davina's plotting. You could not think to take responsibility for her actions."

219

"I left you. Unprotected. I shall never forgive meself." Pacing, he slammed his fist into his chest. Spinning to face her, his misery filling him, he reached out to her. "Can ye ever forgive me?"

Taking hold of his outstretched hand, she kissed it. "Stop. You left me to save the queen. Ye had no way of knowing what would happen. I am only grateful Maisie went to see her cousin. I have nae doubt she would have ended up imprisoned with us. And then I cannot think what might have happened to the bairn."

Sinking down onto the bed, Ian shook his head. "I had no idea she was capable of such acts. I always knew she was defiant and selfish, but to do this…"

"There's a term for it where I come from. Narcissism. Do you know of Narcissus of Greek mythology?"

"Aye. He was the one who fell in love with his reflection."

"Yes. He loved no one but himself. I fear Davina is like that. And now all know the truth aboot her and she will never be able to do this again at Eilean Donan castle."

"We must find her. She cannot go unpunished."

"Yes, my love. And we shall. But tonight, we must make up for time lost." Holding out her arms, he moved against her, clinging to warmth and the love he knew she felt for him. She did not hate him, or feel he was responsible, even though in his heart he would ne'er forgive himself. He was the luckiest man ever born and he would spend every day of his life showing her how much she meant to him.

Passion borne of guilt, gratitude, and love burned his lips as they captured hers. Running his hands over her body, he quickly managed to relieve her of her clothes, shedding his at the same time. All he could think was pressing his flesh against hers, burying himself deep within her, melting into her. Never had he felt anything akin to this. He who prided himself on having fear of naught, this frightened him—this overwhelming need to have her with him.

Thirsting for her as a man starving, he kissed every inch of her body and, when she thrust her hips against him, begging for release, he took her with all the love and desire and need that consumed him.

Chapter Twenty

The games were set to begin in a week and the castle folk were busier than ever. The fields were set up for games of skill, agility and speed, and the courtyard for a dance competition. There would be a marketplace where craftsmen could show off their wares and booths for food and drink.

Although there was still some tension remaining among the clans, since it was difficult to put aside years of competition and animosity, Skye was determined that all would enjoy the festivities. She managed to be everywhere— despite still being tired from her near-death ordeal—helping, encouraging, asking questions. Her excuse for her lack of experience was she had been raised in France and these games were specific to Scotland. Looking forward to it all helped her bad memories to fade.

Neasa was right when she said they were bonded after their experience. Together they planned menus and made arrangements and oversaw all the activities, Neasa instructing her in the proper way to do things, as a mother would teach her daughter. Still, a pall hung over the clan. There had been no sighting of Davina and many believed she had sought refuge with another clan. It was a popular topic speculating what yarns she had spun to explain why she was no longer with her own clan.

Three days before the games, Skye walked down to the training field. Instantly spying her husband, in all his muscular, sweaty glory, she sidled up to him. Shirtless in the cold autumn air, he looked as comfortable as a man in front of a warm fire. It was all she could do not to find some pretext to tempt him back to their chamber.

Seeing her, he smiled, then paused instructing the men how high to set up a horizontal pole to draw her close. Leaning in, so only she could hear, he whispered, "When ye look at me like that, I can only think to take you to bed."

"My thoughts exactly," she said, grinning.

"Laird, this high?" one of the men called out.

"Can ye hold the thought for a short time?" he asked her, his tone expressing his disappointment.

"Yes. If you tell me what all the games are to be and how they are played. I hae been so busy with other preparations, I have not had time to come down here and ask."

Scottish pride showed in his smile. "This one," he said, pointing to the bar, is for the sheaf toss. A bundle of straw is wrapped in a bag and tossed over the bar."

"That doesnae sound so difficult."

"The straw weighs aboot a stone."

Studying British history had taught her to convert stones to pounds, so he was saying about twenty pounds. Not so easy. Nodding, she acknowledged the difficulty.

"And we can also use metal balls instead of straw, weighing aboot four stone."

Impressive. "And that?" she asked, pointing to some long, tapered, heavy wooden poles.

"The caber toss. A man must balance it on one end and run forward, and toss it end over end so it lands facing away."

223

Smiling up at her husband, she asked coyly, "And which is your event, my strong and handsome man?"

Shrugging humbly, he shook his head. "Would it impress ye if I won one or two?"

"You need do naught more to impress me. But I do think you should come to our chamber and remind me how much I desire your body."

"Keep going, men," he called out. "I'll be back."

Trying not to giggle when several of the other men cleared their throats pointedly, Skye led the way up the hill and into the main hall.

As they entered, a flying Maisie ran into Skye's arms. "Thank the good Lord you are safe. This was all me fault. I never should have left you." Moving slightly away, Maisie angled her head to her brother. "Have ye found the bitch? Because I would love a go at her before she is drawn and quartered."

Both men reacted with raised eyebrows to Maisie's sentiments. She was a gentle soul who always tried to find the best in people. Skye laughed out loud. "Remind me to never get on yer bad side," she teased.

Maisie took hold of her hand and led her to one of the benches as Skye looked over at her husband with regret. Their play would have to wait. As they sat, Maisie looked Skye up and down. "You are well? Yer arm?"

"Healed. I am quite well and looking forward to the upcoming games."

Looking at Ian, Maisie shook her head. "You have marrit a very brave wummin. I do nae think I could have survived such a trial."

"How is your cousin? And yer bairn?"

Maisie grinned. "Claray brought a fine, strapping boy into the world. They are both healthy. My own bairn

224

has started to think of me ribs as targets." She laughed at her own jest. "And I was preparing to return home when Errol brought me the news. Can you ever forgive me?"

"There is naught to forgive. You had no hand in her evil."

"But I regret leaving you alone here. I thought you were safe, that the wife of the laird would have no problem running the castle with Neasa's help. It ne'er occurred to me Neasa would be taken as well. How does she fare?"

"We are both recovered. Thanks to Freya and Kenna. They risked much to bring us sustenance and blankets."

"And medicine," Ian added.

Maisie lifted an eyebrow in question. "Medicine?"

"Aye. French medicine. It stopped the plague and rid me of the poison in my arm."

"Plague?" Errol cried, rushing over to his wife.

"It is safe now. Rory sickened after helping Davina, but she unwittingly saved the clan by sending him across to the stables to die. Then Skye had Freya give him her medicine and he recovered. No one else has showed signs of the disease."

"How much I missed in so short a time." She angled her head to Skye. "Do you have more of this magic medicine?"

"It is a kind of magic, I suppose. But, no, I fear it is gone."

"Can we send to France for more?" Maisie asked.

Skye had not thought of this possibility. She had to think quickly. "We can try. I will write to the doctor who gave it to me. It was too late to save my mother and father, but luckily I kept it."

Skye prayed they would forget about the medicine. In the meantime, she could address a letter to an unknown doctor in France and then say he never responded. Tension tightened her muscles as she recalled the old saying that when you tell one lie you must tell three more to cover it. How long would she be able to keep her secret?

***

The other clans arrived in force. Frasers, Mackintosh, Mackay, Murray, Forbes, Cameron, and Munro. Even the Earls, Moray, Atholl, and Morton, who had commanded at the last battle arrived with relatives. Happily, many brought food and drink, since feeding thousands would be impossible if the MacKenzies had to provide alone for all.

The women competed for the most fashionable gowns and the young girls practiced in the hall for the dance competition. The sound of bagpipes echoed off the walls and spilled outside into the courtyard.

Men walked around the training yard, sizing up the events and deciding which to compete in. And the overall feeling was one of joy and exuberance. With such energy, it was not difficult to let go of the unpleasantness that had nearly cost her life. But in her heart, Skye knew fate could not be so cruel as to bring her all this way only to lose her life abandoned and in the dark.

All enmity between the clans was set aside in favor of the celebration. They had come together to defeat those who threatened and denigrated their queen and they had been victorious. Not one of them was lost in the fray, while the rebels suffered casualties, their leader dying suddenly and soundlessly as defeat loomed.

It was amazing to Skye that these men and women

could be enemies one day and come together the next when bound by a common threat. Happy that these days would be made up of friendly competition, Skye flitted about, trying desperately to remember names and faces and make friends of the other wives. As wife of the laird, she commanded respect and the other women immediately accepted her. Raised as a loner, with Harper as her only friend, Skye was nearly overwhelmed with all the compliments and attention. Deciding it was something she could get accustomed to, she was also aware that this camaraderie between the clans would not last.

Ian competed in the axe throw and archery. Holding her breath as he stepped up and took aim at the targets, the crowd yelled encouragement. The axe fell just short of the center, but it was the closest of all the others. One of the Frasers landed an arrow in the bullseye, to great shouts of appreciation. Then Ian stepped up and his arrow split the other. The people erupted in amazement and Skye fairly burst with pride.

Slapping each other on the back, the men sought refreshment as the other events continued. And it was non-stop dancing and singing and music for three days.

Each night Ian and Skye fell into their bed, exhausted but joyous. The festival was a great success, and they were delighted. The memory of what Davina had done still hung over them, and threatened to dampen the celebration. The woman had not been found and Ian wondered if one of the clans had taken her in and believing some lie she had concocted. Skye knew the woman had great powers of persuasion, especially with the opposite sex. Hopefully, someone would come forward and expose her. Until then, Skye had no doubt she was planning revenge for her failure to rid herself of Skye.

227

***

The entertainment was winding down and the clans were gathering their things to return home. Winter's breath would soon turn the landscape harsh, and the Scots knew enough to seek the warmth of their homes before the permeating cold struck.

Ian was standing in the door frame, looking out onto the courtyard, and eating a bannock when the laird of clan Murray approached him.

"We thank ye for yer hospitality, Ian. This has been a celebration that will long be remembered."

"It was my pleasure. I am a lucky mon."

"I can see that. Yer bride is most comely and that is why I find it hard to believe what I have heard."

Ian's attention was instantly focused on the other man. "And what is that?"

"That she stole you from one more deserving and tried to kill her rival."

His chin rising at this, Ian's eyes narrowed at the Murray. "I take it you have heard the lies of one who is the devil's spawn."

"That lovely lass. Why she is all softness and tears."

"And so you have offered her shelter?" Ian was trying desperately to control the rage lashing him. Davina's wiles were effective and could not blame the other man for his weakness at a woman's charms.

Angling his head, Ian led the other man into the main hall, now mostly deserted. Sitting on one of the benches, Ian called for mugs of ale, which were instantly delivered. When they were alone again, Ian took a deep breath. "Tell me all that has transpired."

"Can I count on ye to be fair? The pur lass has suffered so."

Vibrating now with unspent fury, Ian forced himself to remain calm. "Hae you ever known me to be aught but fair?"

"Nay. You are an honorable man. Even your enemies acknowledge that." The Murray squared his shoulders. "The lass came knocking at our gates, her clothing torn, her cheeks streaked with signs of her misery. It was as I said. She told us a stranger had appeared and, using witchcraft and terrible spells, managed to steal her betrothed. She was thrown out of her home and left to fend for herself. I couldnae in good conscience turn her away,"

"Where is she now?"

"At my home. She begged me not to appeal to you, saying you were so bewitched you would seek only to silence her. So I must tell ye she is now under my protection."

Wordlessly, Ian rose and motioned with his hands for the other laird to stay seated. Swallowing the words he wished to fling at the other man, he instead went to the corridor leading to the kitchen. "Freya, Kenna, Sorcha, Alba, Isla," he shouted. "Come into the main hall now."

The five women immediately appeared, waiting to hear what the laird desired. "I wish you to tell laird Murray about Davina."

Sorcha spit into the rushes. "She is a demon from hell. She forced us to imprison our lady and Neasa in the dungeon and they nearly died."

Freya stepped up. "She has been naught but a torment to us her whole life. She plotted to marry to the laird and would use any means to gain the vows from him."

Now it was Kenna's turn. "She brought potatoes into our kitchen after forcing one of the stableboys to get them from a *Francach* soldier. The soldier gave him the plague

229

and if it wasn't for our lady, the terrible sickness would have killed us all."

As the women spoke, the Murray's mouth gaped open. When they finished, he turned to Ian. "I hae been a fool. Me wife is gone these two years and Davina promised herself to me. She is a bonnie lass, and I was too easily beguiled. Can you forgive me for doubting your integrity?"

"Aye. I know what it is to be lonely, and I understand how easily a man can fall."

"What shall I do with her?"

"She needs to answer for her crimes. Secure her with binds and bring her here. She is ours to deal with."

"I will see to it as soon as I return home."

Ian turned to the women. "Thank ye all for yer words. Davina nearly claimed another victim. But we will see an end to her evil ways.

***

The quiet in the castle was unnerving after the crowds had departed. Ian and Skye climbed the steps to their chamber, Skye's cheeks aching from smiling so much. No sooner was the door closed than Ian swept her up and carried her to the bed.

"Why, my lord, have you any energy left after the activities of the past days?" she teased.

"I will ne'er be too tired to touch you, *mo ghradh*." And he pulled her to him, delighting in the feel of her soft curves against him. "But there is something I must tell you."

The tone of his voice told her it was not to be a casual comment. "What is amiss?"

"Nay. It is good news. Davina sought sanctuary with clan Murray. At first she had the laird convinced she was the wronged one, but a few of the clanswomen here set him straight."

"Now what?" A thousand possibilities crowded in.

"He will bring her here to face her punishment. So, it will be up to you and Neasa to decide."

Skye blew out a breath. "She is dangerous, Ian. But I cannot condemn another to death."

"It is what she deserves."

"I could not live with myself, but we must devise a plan that protects the clan from her vile ways."

"Hae I mentioned how much I love ye?" he asked softly.

"Ye can ne'er tell me too much." Gently, she pressed her lips to his. "We should sleep and think on this more in the morning."

"Sleep? Ah, yes, *mo chridhe*. But first there is something I am pressed to do."

Before she could ask what, his hands were caressing her, all thoughts gone from her head except his touch.

Chapter Twenty-One

So many visitors had left the castle in need of cleaning. Days were spent putting all in order, but thoughts of Davina returning were never far from Skye's mind. A punishment equal to her transgressions, short of execution, was not a simple thing.

The morning after Ian had told her about Davina, she sought advice from Neasa. After all, the other woman had suffered the same as she and was entitled to an opinion.

They talked at length, but no solution presented. And it was several days later that a missive came from clan Murray. He was sorry, but Davina had realized her subterfuge had failed and had run before they could detain her. The idea that she was somewhere free was more than troubling, but there was some comfort knowing she could not approach the castle without the guards seeing her. Still, it was unsettling to imagine what she would do next.

And there was still the matter of the cloak. Skye and several of the other ladies had searched high and low and found no trace of it. They did find more of her gowns, several of which had been slashed to pieces. The only reassuring part was that Davina could have no knowledge of the cloak's power. Skye could not imagine the havoc she could wreak in the twenty-first century. Then again, the technology alone would be virtually impossible for her to absorb. She would have no money, no friends, no understanding of life. Unless, for some reason, she managed to meet Harper. But that was completely out of the realm of possibility, wasn't it?

Clearly, Davina had to know she no longer had a chance to wed either Ian or Laird Murray, but that did not mean she would not try for another useful conquest. And it wasn't as if they could get on the internet to the other clans and send out a warning. But with luck, she would stay far away from Eilean Donan.

Days passed with no sign of trouble and the castle settled into the quiet workings of daily life. Each day, Skye found Ian a constant source of joy and her new life hundreds of years in the past was everything she could have hoped for and more.

With her history, she feared that good things must come to an end, but each hour reassured her that all was well. She no longer thought of the everyday luxuries she had left behind, like running water and microwaves. This life was simpler, and she found herself immersed in the joy of everyday tasks.

Christmas approached and Skye was trying to decide what to give Ian. She did not sew, and she actually had no coin of her own, so she was thinking of baking him something special. Recipes swirled in her head and as she settled in to sleep on one cold night, snuggled up against the warm, hard body of the husband she adored, she finally decided on a cake made with chocolate. Kenna would know where she could procure the special ingredient. Hoping she would please him, she drifted off into a peaceful dream.

The dream, though, quickly turned into a nightmare. She was in her chamber, wrapped in a blanket. Beside her, Ian lay lifeless, his arm outstretched as if he had tried to protect her before he succumbed. His lifeblood stood out in stark relief on the white linen. Suddenly, a demon rose up, dagger in hand. She could hear the air move as the weapon slashed through it, aiming at her heart.

Screaming, she jolted upright, soaked in sweat. There, in the corner, lurked the demon from her vision. Standing, it moved close to her, its hissing voice striking terror in her. But, before it could strike, Ian dove across the bed and wrestled it to the ground. An eerie screech rattled the walls as they struggled.

Unsure how to help him, Skye watched as Ian bested the thing. A groan rattled its chest as it struggled to get air. Ian stood and Skye raced over to jump into his arms. "Are ye hurt?"

"Nay. But if you hadn't cried out, she would have killed us while we slept."

She? And then Skye immediately knew the identity of the demon. Davina could not accept she had been bested and sought retribution. "Is she dead?"

Ian lit several candles, and it was obvious who had attacked them. It was also evident she was injured, but still lived.

The chamber door was flung open and Conall and Daimh rushed in. Seeing Davina on the ground, they immediately knew what had happened.

"Are you well, Laird," Daimh asked.

"Aye. But she might need tending."

Conall reached for her, but she pulled away. "Do nae touch me," she snarled. She angled her head to Skye. "Ye see what I am wrapped in? It is your cloak. I ken it is of value to ye, and I intend to burn it. I will take all from ye 'ere I die."

"The cloak has no value. And you have done

234

enough." Unsure what power the cloak still had, Skye wanted it away from Davina. It had promised to return to where Skye had started, and then Davina would be completely out of their reach and at the mercy of the future. Again, thoughts of the other woman in the twenty-first century unnerved Skye.

Davina's blood soaked into a corner of the worn fabric, and, at Skye's words, she wrapped herself tighter in it. "Fear not, my lady," she scoffed. "I will prevail. The future is mine."

At her words, Davina managed to get up and race into the corridor. The men followed her, running down the steps and searching the immediate area, but she had disappeared into thin air. The men's shuffled back to Ian's bedchamber. "Davina is gone," Conall said, disbelief in his tone.

"Where did she go?" Ian demanded.

"She is a witch. But there is no other explanation," Ian whispered. The other men nodded their agreement.

"The question is, where did she go?" Ian repeated. Skye was afraid she knew the answer, but now that Davina was labeled a witch, she dare not explain. Not that they would believe her anyway. It occurred to her she was now in 1562 Scotland forever and the thought filled her with joy. There was still that niggling worry that Davina might somehow encounter Harper or someone to help her adjust to her new circumstances, but Skye knew that was now out of her control.

Shaking their heads, the men left the chamber. Ian stood up and he, too, was baffled. "The folklore teaches that ofttimes there is no explanation. I suppose if there is white magic, there must also be black. But she is gone, and we can pray it is for good."

Moving back to the bed, he wrapped Skye in his arms and held her close. "The day you came into me life, it was indeed magic, and I give you my word, I shall always be grateful, *mo ghradh*."

"And I shall always love you."

Epilogue

Walking into the beautiful cottage on the loch, Harper Forbes finally appreciated why her best friend, Skye, wanted to come here. Outside, Eilean Donan Castle gleamed in the early morning sun, painted with golds and pinks and blues and reflecting in the water surrounding it. It was like looking at a dream within a dream.

After receiving Skye's cryptic note and then hearing no more, Harper was too pragmatic to let it go without an explanation. Hence her trip here to Dornie and the castle. She wanted some answers as to what had happened to her friend, and she had no intention of leaving without them.

Walking into the bathroom to wash her face after the long journey, she was startled by a cry from the bedroom. Rushing out into the next room, she was stunned to see a young woman dressed in medieval clothes and wrapped in a filthy old cloak.

Harper recognized that cloak. Skye had shown it to her before she left.

"Where?" the woman squeaked.

"It's not possible," Harper replied. "There has to be a logical explanation."

TURN THE PAGE FOR AN EXCERPT OF
Follow Me

Harper Forbes embarks on a journey of a lifetime as she follows her friend to Scotland, only to discover that she, too, been mysteriously transported back in time to the 1500s. In this unfamiliar and perilous world, Harper must navigate through dangers and challenges she never could have imagined. But amidst the chaos and uncertainty, she finds not only her friend but also a love that transcends time itself. What will fate have in store for her? Join Harper on an unforgettable adventure filled with romance, danger, and the timeless power of true love.

Follow Me

AWARD WINNING AUTHOR

LESLIE HACHTEL

Chapter One

Harper Forbes punched in the entry code on the quaint cottage's front door. Unaccustomed to the damp cold, she was anxious to get inside. Turning back to see the view and the shimmering lochs, she finally appreciated why her best friend Skye wanted to come here. And the castle! Eilean Donen above the dark waters was breathtaking.

It had been a long trip but worry over her friend's disappearance fueled Harper through the journey. Now she was in a foreign country, alone, knowing no one. She refused to let that intimidate her. There were so many questions and Harper needed answers.

The risk was that everything Harper had ever believed about reality might be wrong and she was still debating the merits of actually being here in the first place. Time travel? Seriously? It was a ridiculous concept, but then what had happened to her friend? They were so close, more like sisters, so Harper knew Skye wouldn't just vanish.

It had been weeks since she had received the packages from Skye containing her passport, driver's license, clothes, cash, and even her phone. Skye also sent a cryptic message about the cloak working, and a goodbye. None of it made any sense unless she subscribed to a ludicrous notion about travelling through time. It was more logical that something had happened to her, but then why would she mail those boxes. In fact, some had actually been mailed by the landlord here. After hearing no more for weeks, Harper was too pragmatic to let it go without an explanation.

When she had called the owner of the cottage, the woman Harper spoke to agreed it was strange Skye had her mail the two packages after she left. Harper was told Skye had left very specific instructions. The woman seemed nervous, as if Harper was looking to blame her for something done wrong, but Harper reassured the woman she just wanted some answers as to what had happened to her friend.

Initial concern had built to an urgency and hence her trip here to Dornie and the castle. Now that she had made the trip here, she had no intention of leaving without a viable reason for Skye's disappearance. But the idea of time travel was not in Harper's lexicon. The unknown twirled around in her mind like the wheel in a hamster's cage.

In addition to the worry, Harper missed Skye and found it hard to shake the sadness after she left Memphis. Learning many years ago that action tended to lift the grey smoke of depression, Harper had decided to get on a plane. Her logical side reminded her it might be useless. There were some things she simply couldn't control or discover. Then again, what could a small getaway hurt even if she couldn't find Skye?

Harper had received those packages and it convinced her that Skye had either completely lost herself in fantasy or—and was this even conceivable—had actually traveled back in time. But if Skye had arranged to have her things sent to Harper, where was she now? And how was she managing without identification or money? In 1562? Again—seriously?

Harper set down her luggage and took a moment to appreciate the bungalow. Spacious and cozy at the same time, the accommodations here were welcoming. Plaid shades on the windows were raised to frame the magnificent view of the rolling hills and she was certain that come spring, the fields would boast vivid emerald-green. Of course, she'd be home by then. Unbidden, a chill ran up her spine, but Harper shook it off.

Eilean Donan Castle gleamed in the distance, the ancient walls painted with the golds of the late morning sunshine and reflected in the water surrounding it. It was like looking at a dream within a dream. Yes, that summed it up. A few sparse trees sheltered the stones, which made the edifice even more imposing and unassailable. It was as if it declared "if you are foe, you will not reach us". Exciting and foreboding and promising.

This all started when Skye had found a portrait of a Scotsman painted in the 1500s and she had apparently fallen in love with the man, or at least his image. A little research and it was clear the background of the picture was here, with a backdrop of the castle. Declaring the man her soul mate and determined to find him, Skye had bought a time travel cloak on Ebay, of all places. She could hear Skye now: "their purchases come with a guarantee". Ridiculous! But Skye was not to be talked out of it and had come here, to Eilean Donan castle. And soon after, after sending Harper packages with her belongings and identification, she vanished. That was nearly two months ago. Now it was approaching the winter holidays and that was definitely not Harper's favorite time of the year. If she was being honest, she was looking for an excuse to think about something—anything—else other than "deck the halls". She and Skye had always made sure to spend this time of year together, even when Harper was briefly married, because neither of them had family to speak of, or any warm memories to look back on. So, Skye wouldn't just disappear, especially at Christmastime.

Harper was beyond worried about her friend, the fear and the loneliness, a sharp stick pressing against her heart.

Even with her crazy imagination, Skye was the best friend Harper had ever had. Her fantasies and fairy tales were always stretching the bounds of reality, while Harper was earthbound and practical. Skye's idea of catapulting through time was absurd. But when you eliminated the impossible... was it truly impossible?

Harper picked up her bag and carried it into the bedroom. She'd unpack later. She wanted to wash her face after the long journey.

Harper took a long look in the bathroom mirror above the sink. "Who are you?" she asked the reflection. "Chasing after Skye because she said she could time travel? You know better than that!" Harper sighed. "But where is she?" There was no quelling the constant worry.

A woman's cry carried from the bedroom. Harper immediately startled at the sound of panic in the woman's howl. Rushing out into the next room, she was stunned to see a young woman she didn't recognize dressed in medieval clothes and wrapped in a filthy old cloak. The woman's dark hair floated around her in a mass of tangles and the expression on her face was a combination of confusion and distress. Gauging her to be in her early twenties, the woman nevertheless had the look of one who had seen much of life. Her gown was impressively authentic, and her stance defiant, her hands on her hips, her eyes narrowed.

How did this woman get in here? Who was she? Or maybe—maybe—it was all meant to make visitors feel as if they had gone back in time. Part of the atmosphere? Still… it was odd.

Harper might have been annoyed by the intrusion, until her gaze was drawn again to the cloak the woman wore. Harper recognized that cloak. Skye had shown it to her before she left for Scotland. There was no mistaking it had to be the same one. Now more questions buzzed through Harper's mind: how was it this other woman was wearing it? Who was she? Did she mug Skye and steal it? But who would bother robbing anyone for an old rag of a garment? Or was it that jet lag caused hallucinations?

Harper was pretty sure the woman was real and not a figment of her imagination, but how did she just appear here? Harper was certain she locked the front door when she arrived. And did she have any information about what had happened to Skye? Before she could ask anything, the other woman momentarily flashed her gaze at Harper before angling her head and scanning the room.

"Where?" the woman demanded, irritation twisting her features. "What happened?" Her gaze direct and her lips puckered, she glared at Harper as if Harper was responsible. "Did ye bewitch me?" The rancor in her tone was unmistakable.

"What I'm thinking—not possible," Harper said aloud more to herself than to her intruder. "There has to be a logical explanation."

The stranger took several steps away from Harper, but she was too busy looking everywhere at once to answer.

More curious than intimidated, Harper took a step forward. "Who are you? And how did you get in here?"

"This isnae the castle. How *did* I get here? Indeed.

How did ye do it?" Her brows came together, forming a crease between her dark eyes—eyes that reflected a lack of empathy. Her tone softened. "Ye must be verra rich to live in this place."

"I don't live here," Harper responded instinctively. "I'm looking for my friend Skye."

"Skye?" The woman fairly shrieked. "Skye?" she repeated. "That *howfin galla*." Even Harper, who spoke little Gaelic, guessed that a *galla* was a bitch by the venom in the other woman's tone.

"So you know her! Where is she?" Finally, some answers!

"No doubt bewitching the laird—who is mine!" Her reptilian smile made goosebumps rise on Harper's skin. "Make no mistake. I will end her." This last was said on a breathy whisper seething with malice. The woman continued to smile without humor, her eyes also reminding Harper of a snake. "If ye are friends of the lady Skye"—she spit the name as if it tasted like lemons— "and if she is yer caraid, ye are no caraid of mine," she said. "So do tell—who are ye?" the woman demanded, her voice again more a screech.

Harper raised her eyebrows and, determining to stand her ground, stared at the other woman. "I might ask the same of you."

"Davina. Of Clan Mackenzie." This was said with a lifted chin and a thick Scottish brogue.

This was too fantastic to be anything but a hallucination, but that didn't make sense, either. Harper decided that maybe she should just play along. "It is possible I have a problem with her as well. Where is she?"

"And who be ye?" the one named Davina of Clan MacKenzie repeated, annoyance clear in her tone.

"I am Harper of—Clan Forbes. I suppose you expect me to welcome you to the twenty-first century." It just seemed the right thing to say, which was silly.

"The what?" Her puzzlement actually appeared genuine.

"I believe that cloak you are wearing is responsible." *But really, was it?* "It belongs to Skye. Where did you get it?"

About the Author

Leslie Hachtel has been working since she was fifteen and her various jobs have included licensed veterinary technician, caterer, horseback riding instructor for the disabled and advertising media buyer, which have all given her a wealth of experiences.

However, it has been writing that has consistently been her passion. She is an award-winning and Amazon best-selling author who has written seventeen romance novels, including twelve historicals and five romantic suspense.

Leslie lives in Florida with her very supportive husband, and her new writing buddy, Josie, the poodle mix.

She loves to hear from readers!

Website: https://www.lesliehachtel.com/

Facebook:
https://www.facebook.com/lesliehachtelwriter/

Twitter: @lesliehachtel

Blog: http://lesliehachtelwriter.wordpress.com

Bookbub:
https://www.bookbub.com/authors/leslie-hachtel

www.ingramcontent.com/pod-product-compliance
Lightning Source LLC
Chambersburg PA
CBHW021233250626
47155CB00008B/2999